Momentary Aberrations

Momentary Aberrations

Tom Cardamone

REBEL SATORI PRESS
New Orleans & New York

Published in the United States of America by
REBEL SATORI PRESS
www.rebelsatoripress.com

Cover design by Sven Davisson
Cover image: *Warminiaen*, c. 1618, artist unknown, courtesy of the
Rijksmuseum, Amsterdam, the Netherlands.

ISBN: 978-1-60864-407-0

A few of these stories have been previously published:
"A Seppuku of Centerfolds," *KGB Bar Literary Review*, edited by
Christopher Stoddard, 2019; "Bent on Midnight Frolic," *Unspeakable
Horror 2: Abominations of Desire*, edited by Vince A. Liaguno,
Evil Jester Press, 2017; "Double Feature," Circlet Press Halloween
Microfiction blog, October 31st, 2020; "Grey Salamanders," *Gents:
Steamy Stories from the Age of Steam*, edited by Matthew Bright, Lethe
Press, 2018; "Hypoxyphilia," *Nasty: Fetish Fights Back*, edited by
Anna Yeatts and Chris Philips, Flash Fiction Online, 2017; "Some
Nights in Kyoto," *Spunk Magazine*, #11, edited by Aaron Tilford,
2016; "Recall the Creature," *Spunk Magazine*, #15, edited by Aaron
Tilford, 2023

O Rose thou art sick.
The invisible worm,
That flies in the night
In the howling storm:

Has found out thy bed
Of crimson joy:
And his dark secret love
Does thy life destroy.

—William Blake
The Sick Rose

*My deepest gratitude to Sven Davisson
for calling our brethren together.*

Platter of Perversities

Introduction

This is my third short story collection and the other two both had aborted introductions, written but not included in the final version. I grew up voraciously reading science fiction and fantasy, genres perhaps best suited for the short form. Occasionally, those cheap, worn paperback collections would include introductions by the author, and even commentary for each story. I only sometimes found them satisfactory, however. I promised myself that if I ever realized my dream of becoming a published author, I would avoid introductions or explanatory matter: let the work speak for itself, here, here! Well fuck all that. The first time my then-boyfriend-now-husband and I held hands was on the street one sunny afternoon in Carroll Gardens, Brooklyn. We'd always been reticent about public displays of affection but it seemed so necessary at that specific moment: we were looking at buying an apartment not too far away, we hadn't yet moved in together (a rarity in New York City, after more than a decade of dating -possibly one of the reasons why we have lasted so long) and I wanted that: fingers interlocked -we deserved the casual closeness that belonged to the surrounding straight couples. No sooner had we clasped hands then one of three boys across the street threw a rock at my head. My husband Leo expertly caught that rock in mid-air and instinctively whipped it back at them. They shot in every direction like startled birds. My heart pounded. Every molecule of my being united in one vibrating exhalation: *I will marry him*. My next thought: *and if I ever do drag, I'm going to call myself Carroll Gardens*.

1

Not long after my second short story collection, *Night Sweats: Tales of Homosexual Wonder and Woe*, was published, we were married on the beach in Venice California. (Dig that Poe-like subtitle, and I've always been fascinated by the word *homosexual*, so clinical and medical yet implying public sex, overheated immorality, and perhaps *the* best single reason to dodge the draft.) My best friend Kate officiated. We decided to get married outside, under the sun, a public display of our love. The ocean gleamed as we exchanged our vows. A month or two later, we flew South for a relative's wedding. At a dinner beforehand I was introduced to the baptistevangelicalchristiandemagogue who would be officiating the wedding. His handshake was so limp, he practically recoiled. My initial thought was that he must be sick and self-conscious about sharing his infection. At the wedding the next night, he mounted the stage and, glowering at the two of us, shouted "We all know that marriage is *only* between a man and a woman, regardless these momentary aberrations." After the ceremony I rushed to the bathroom and downloaded Grindr. I was so sure I would find him there. Faceless profile and brief DL description. Cock sucking bottom. To no avail, alas. The enemy is *not* us, not some thwarted, closeted version of ourselves that we can easily understand and dismiss. They are there from a young age, craving our collective deaths. Theirs is an apocalyptic fantasy, and we can't be drawn in.

I put my phone in my jacket pocket and elbowed my way to the front of the bar, furious, silent, isolated in a cheerful crowd. I don't know how long it took before I realized that I had the title to my next short story collection, but I remember that I smiled at the thought. Aberrant, momentary, as vacillating as life itself. The waning fantasies and callous intentions of their petty death cult don't matter. What matters is that we find each other on the dancefloor, we sing our own songs, we march down summer streets, we write our stories and read them aloud.

Gold Elevator

Nondescript office building (are there any other kinds?) and a long hallway and a stairwell behind a door marked "Exit" and in the basement, an elevator. The elevator only goes down. You don't know how many subterranean floors hover beneath the skyscraper above. You only know that the elevator is strikingly gold. Clean and polished, it inspires a sense of solidity, value, and trust that is the opposite of your journey. It has room for only one passenger. Purposeful in design; you *should* be alone before the doors open, alone with your decision to enter an underworld formed fully of desire, alone to question yourself, to weigh the risks while encased in gold, an invaluable sinking coffin of unfathomable worth.

You exit the gold elevator when the doors open, more out of habit than a tactic, a commitment to your decision to visit this place, to plunge in. It doesn't really have a name, does it? It's referred to as "the club," or "going down." "So. Have you gone down, yet?" Certain nighttime dwellers ask one another this question while smoking cigarettes or limp joints in grimy basement sex clubs beneath Sunset Park overpasses or among the torn seats of the city's last porno theater in Jackson Heights. It's an anonymous question asked on sex apps amongst faceless profiles who have already answered the question, *What are you into* with *anything goes*. It's a question, but it's also a test.

You already paid the doorman twenty dollars, or fifty or one hundred, he doesn't make change, to gain entry. He copped your phone and slipped it into a Ziploc plastic baggie, so no pictures, no recording, no texting, no video games.

You exit and blink at the bright fluorescent light. Usually, such dens of inequity are dark affairs; this one, however, is a surprise that sets you back on your heels. But the smell pulls you in, the male sweat of exertion and the even more powerful damp pungency of urine. On either side of the hall, an endless row of nineteenth-century porcelain urinals. These uniform behemoths appear as if large bathtubs turned on end. You can step into them for a semblance of privacy. They are certainly old, webbed with cerulean cracks that practically glow from having absorbed the acidity of decade after decade of corrosive piss. The tiled floor seems slippery, so you proceed with caution. This gallery of urinals goes on and on. Your mind drifts from carnal thoughts as you marvel at this remarkable feat of engineering. *Was this an abandoned subway tunnel? Surely, I've traveled several blocks by now. . .* The sound of running water gives you pause. The closest urinal has recently been flushed. Gold water dilutes at the basin; the warmth of the previous occupant still shimmers in the air. Your penis extends as you unbuckle to take his place. There's a large pubic hair curled on the white rim of the urinal. It's so thick you wonder if it's human. Your exposed cock lengthens further as you lean down to pluck up the hair. The tear-like follicle pearls with a singular drop of piss. You place it on your tongue. The sting of urine in your mouth erupts across your tastebuds. Your erection is complete. Your erection is divine, totemic. You teethe on the giant hair and hope to absorb its darkness, stain your lust so black no misgivings seep through, all possible regrets drown in a night tide. Your heart is beating at the idea of kneeling before the beast who shed such hair. You imagine the forcefulness of the unbridled piss he had taken, what must have been only moments before your arrival. Dropping to your knees, you place your cheek against the porcelain inner cavity, still warm from his powerful stream. You long to bathe in his maleness, to surrender to his flow. To drink from his strong body. You strip and kick your clothes away to better nest in the concave womb. You drink from the rivulets of water streaming down, wishing it were him, or a huddle of men unknown to you, alternately releasing their fluids into your mouth: piss, semen, spit, a drop or two of blood squeezed out of fresh cuts from hands wounded during the day's labor. The lights dim as the porcelain glows. The thin blue fissures that lace this private interior expand like veins. You put your hands out to steady yourself and meet membranous resistance. You are in an egg filling up with a warm, globular liquid, and as you gulp for breath, it fills your mouth. It tastes like every cock you've ever sucked, warm flesh released from dirty underwear, pasty from droplets of urine and a layer of sweat, from being manhandled by nicotine-stained fingers. It tastes like the life you always wanted, what has until now been just out of reach, and you gulp it down as the egg begins to spin and the lights go out.

You think of the Minotaur in the labyrinth. Stories everyone knows. How many know the story of those who want to be lost? That the sensation of being lost is, for a chosen few, greater than that of being found? Perversely, you think of co-workers at times like this. That you will have the piss-stained slacks dry-cleaned, same for the shirt splattered with the semen of countless men. The bleached and washed and ironed dress shirt will still retain the nameless white cameos of their sperm, but only you will be able to discern these traces, what looks like folds but rests as dusty fingerprints on the secret shroud of your imperfect disguise. You think of the Minotaur in the labyrinth because the floor has become earthen. The ceiling has rounded out into a tunnel of bedrock and dripping slate. Naked light bulbs hang from exposed wires, placed just far enough apart to light the path but not the tunnel. The tunnel twists and unspools shadow at every step. Naked men cling to each other, tugging at themselves, in huddles of sweaty backs and bobbing heads, some shaved, tattooed, or scarred. You hate that you are thirsty, actually thirsty, not with lust, but your throat is dry with a corporeal thirst, which replaces your desperation to connect, to suck and serve. Even then, you look for a replacement: urine. Some of the surrounding rock is wet. From leaking pipes, the adjacent aquifer? You need the lavatory to place your mouth upturned against the rushing facet, just like when you were a child, dropping your bike on the lawn and rushing into the kitchen as the screen door slams shut. You've always been feeding, eh? Drawing sustenance from any available tap. Even so driven, you linger at the couplings, the throbbing threesomes in shadow, and eye musculature, buttocks, and rooting fingers, admiring the grip on certain throats.

There's a doorway with a neon sign ahead: MEN. You bark a dry laugh. There's certainly no women's restroom down here, so the sign seems pointless and pointed: more the name of an underground city; it should list the fluctuating population. (You once visited a bathhouse in Asia whose website posted the actual number of denizens in real time; the pulsing mutability as men left and entered was as alluring to you as a flickering flame to a moth — a burning whisper: *this* is where you belong.) Another endless row of ancient urinals: the intricate system of crenulated blue cracks as vast and lifegiving as the roots of an immortal tree. Around the corner are stalls with the doors off, running toilets with the seat covers ripped out, white bowls pregnant with turds, cigarette butts, and pearlescent curls of dissolving semen. The sink is running, the faucet broken. You drink like a farm animal, all tongue and unfocused eye. Soothed, lapping away at the surprisingly cold water, you see him lumbering down the hall. Even though it's been years, you remember his gait from that second-floor bathhouse in Hong Kong. He's even gripping the same towel he had there, larger than the cheap, thin ones the sauna provided. You marveled that he would bring his own, that his own comfort and pleasure were so central to his being. Bow-legged, the exaggerated shoulders made from a life of manual labor, you had spied his silhouette in the sauna, holding open his towel so the thin faun-like boy on his knees could cower beneath the girth of the heavy wand rising before him. Engorged, it widened at the end with a mucilaginous foreskin that, even in the winding white clouds of steam, you could see it dribbled with its own globular, internal heat. You had moved in, hoping to replace the quivering youth on the floor. But he ignored you and all comers, letting the curled supplicant feast while the gathering congregation furtively tried to caress his chest and rigid stomach. The sharp bristles of his pubic hair were boar-like, wild, impervious to the humidity that filled the small, musty room. You knew enough to bide your time; he possessed an abundance of masculinity and would spend his seed several times that night. You receded into the shadows to wait, but never glimpsed him again. You were wrong. Perhaps he had to catch a train back to the mainland or had a wife and family to return to. Now here he was, in your city, possibly a tourist, or a recent transplant, naked save that original towel, watching you drink with a quizzical look. His jaw juts out, the thin outline of an emerging beard, the same thick hair as the forest that converges on his cock. He shifts his footing, and the towel parts. The heavy head of his dark penis hangs languidly beneath a scabbard of thick foreskin. The towel drops. You rush to catch it, to keep it from being soiled on the piss-soaked floor. He spreads his arms to grip either side of the doorless latrine, and the coil of black hair that punctures each armpit makes you gasp; that maleness could be composed of such impenetrable darkness -it all makes sense now. You swallow, on your knees, cradling his discarded towel, your face before the heft of his rising cock. It has its own pungent scent, one that could momentarily be disguised by soap but never erased. The smell of hunger in the jungle. He flexes his ample thigh muscles, and old scars inflate. With this signal, you begin to lick his length and watch, eyes wide, for signs of approval or displeasure. He continues to grow in your mouth, and you work it all the way in, filling your throat with his forceful rigidity. You re-position yourself, buttocks on the wet floor, ankles crossed, to be the best receptacle you can possibly be. He moves with you, course pubic hair filling your nostrils and scratching at the corners of your now openly weeping eyes. The first taste of his precum hits the back of your throat, igniting a new fire of delight throughout your entire body. You ejaculate prematurely, without ever touching your own member. No matter, it's his orgasm you seek, yours is but a comma in one sentence, in a lone paragraph in the book he's writing in your mouth. Keep swallowing flesh and breathe out new languages. This is an underground city after all, rooted in an unrecorded culture with plenty of argot to go around, most of which will be forgotten. Still, somewhere in the opposing tunnels you both traversed to join here, someone, generations ago, once wrote your name on the wall.

You wake up in a hospital. You've been strapped to the bed, likely for your own good. Memories of delirious struggle and exasperated masked male nurses blur in your mind, as if your thoughts can only be seen from the window of a speeding train. You're thirsty now, and calmer. There's a button near your hand that, if pushed, you assume will summon a nurse. You desperately need to pee. You wonder if the nurse will be angry with you. Hold a grudge. You couldn't see the nurse's face from the glare of the light and the green face mask. Someone called for the doctor, and a shot was administered. The long needle was displayed before you, as a threat? A warning. Punishment? You remember the pale, muscular arms of the nurse. The strong hands that held you down while more lithe, expert fingers grasped your flaccid cock and inserted the cold catheter. Blinking, your own body is coming into focus. Though a white sheet covers your chest and arms, your naked waist and legs are embarrassingly exposed. The catheter taped to your dick snakes across the mattress and falls under the bed. You become more oriented to the room: there's a clipboard with graphs at the end of the bed. The bathroom door is closed, and the skeleton of an empty hanger rests like a plastic cormorant. There's no window. You really need to piss. You feel the slightest tug at that rubber tube, and possibly hear a whimper from under the bed. You sense a pleading presence there and imagine a restrained form, similar to yours and just as ravenous.

This isn't what I want, you think.

No, but this, *this,* is what wants you.

The Life Crimson

It wasn't until my third encounter with a vampire that I was able to extract my need. This one I went looking for; the prior two had taken me by surprise. That second one in particular was a heart-pounding experience. He chased me down that long tunnel at the High Street subway stop in Brooklyn. It was 3 AM - not a soul in sight. Of course, I wouldn't have run if I hadn't been drunk. His appearance was vampirically deceptive: they often present as homeless; it's so hard for the majority of vampires to support themselves in the current economy with strictly nocturnal employment. Not like their number is extensive, though no census taker is ticking that midnight box. "Their" number. Our number. *How long will my subterfuge hold here?* Someone in the online chat group I used to frequent posted that a large number of vampires were cab drivers in the 60s and 70s, cruising around after dusk, but that the increasing number of late-night drunks and drug users, particularly in the crack-addled 80s, led to vicarious intoxication and an inordinate number of car accidents.

Back to the subway. The coffin narrative is mostly false; vampires *are* subterranean, with a strict preference for tunnels that grant them access to a largess of blood: meaning cities. We've forgotten how many ancient cities had complex sewer systems and passageways for storage, the discrete travels of emperors and empire - evident to tourists now in Rome and Paris. If you want to find a vampire, you need a city with a vast, decaying underground transportation system. It's the primary reason I moved to New York City. (That and I couldn't figure out the work visas for London. Now there's a subway system built alongside ancient Roman era tunnels and medieval culverts aplenty.)

That night I got off the A train, drunk and high from another night at the Roxy. The drugs I had taken were stepped-on too many times; I felt lethargic rather than invigorated, which was why I had left early, before the regularly scheduled surprise performer, always a female singer with a new single dropping, always someone big, a star, either ascendant or descendant, it didn't matter. The predominantly gay audience, pupils dilated from ecstasy, were rapturous regardless.

I was the only one to exit the nearly empty subway car, a sheath of discarded newspaper levitated in the wake of the departing train. An obsidian shadow extracted itself from the farthest corner. As the shadow took on a human shape, I moved quickly toward the exit. My senses were now alert; I assumed it was a mugger, and as his pace quickened, so did mine. I mounted the stairs two at a time. The shape glided behind me, undulating, expanding, and contracting with my fearful, beery breath. I was determined not to look over my shoulder, to pretend that I didn't recognize the threat, that I was merely in a hurry. Still, when I mounted the rickety escalator, I also took the metallic stairs two at a time, and, confident that I was escaping my pursuer, I looked back. To the untrained eye: an insane man, by all appearances living rough, a scarecrow about to rave against some conspiracy or another; he stood his ground at the trash-strewn base. But I saw the shimmer of thirst around his black eyes, noted the extensive jaw, a muscular appendage warped from prolonged feeding. Fangs glinted like dual stars in the aching black galaxy of his permanent longing. Only then did I realize my mistake. I was about to call out, to reverse course and offer myself up, to desperately take that which I needed also, when a burst of loud teens in leather jackets jumped the turnstiles and tumbled down the descending escalator. The beast vanished, alongside my hopes for immortality.

The next morning, my friends all called to tell me that Grace Jones had been the previous night's performer. Everyone called but my drug dealer, Reverend Rick. Reverend Rick, lanky and dour, dressed as a priest and dispensed drugs as if they were holy sacraments. He must have been berated ad nauseam for selling everyone such lame shit. Back to Grace. Pictures in the following nightlife rags, *HX* and *Homo Alert,* showed her wrapped in cellophane as she perfunctorily belted out her latest dance single before marching up and down the bar, growling all of her biggest hits into a bedazzled microphone while kicking over martini glasses.

I also learned from the chat group to be alert for the smell. Vampires, unbeknownst to themselves, apparently smell like death warmed over in the August sun. They smell *bad.* Of feculent rot, clothes unwashed for decades, the steam pouring off of fresh offal. Like stealthy great white sharks cutting through the surf, unaware that their sleek, martial dorsal fin alerts beachgoers up and down the shore to their presence, the stench of the vampire is a retch-inducing signal that they are near. This is something that high-functioning vampires guard against, and the main reason this fact never made its way into the Victorian penny dreadfuls - those cheap novels that shape the majority of false lore informing popular film and fiction -is that it's not in keeping with their romantic reputation. (Little about them is.) High-functioning, now there's a phrase. In particular, this refers to the rare vampires that have procured steady income and housing, two elevating streams of subsistence that are out of reach for most of their demonic brethren. First of all, you need one to maintain the other, and, just like the majority of humanity, rare is the inherently wealthy vampire. What works against them, most of all, is their overpowering thirst. The desire to hunt and feed eventually eclipses all sense of propriety. The more factually informative members of the chat group, always Russian (from Moscow, always Moscow. Long winter nights plus a deep network of subways) explain to the newbies (and anyone who will listen, they're a dreary, garrulous bunch), that the life expectancy of a vampire is on the average perversely short; once they "take to ground" as they say, this entombed existence is not only bereft of bathing opportunities, but often consists of sleeping in less than sanitary conditions, meaning exposure to sewage, not changing clothes for years at a time. You cannot only smell them coming but will likely vomit before you see them. Their primary food source is almost always out of reach, and they are reduced to supping on disease-ridden rats -wasting away until a form of hunger-induced dementia triggers a level of risk-taking adverse to their survival. Any time you read about a subway track fire in the New York Post, it's more likely than not that a vampire blinded by famine was lured to a sewer grate by the sweet sounds of children skipping rope and burst into flame as the serrated sunlight painted its hollowed cheeks.

Back to Grace Jones. I should dress as her for Halloween next year. A zombie Grace Jones: *Grave Jones*. If only I could sing. Her version of "La Vie en Rose" is perhaps my favorite song. Play that number at my funeral as they lower me into the ground.

Whom am I kidding? Vampires don't have funerals. We only have weddings. And we don't marry each other; we marry the night. A wedding with only one vow. I should go as Lady Gaga next Halloween, instead. I love the Halloween Parade in the West Village. It's the only time we can roam the streets and bare our fangs and act out in public. It's also the only time we ever run into one another, always a frightening affair; what are we going to do, exchange numbers, become friends, get together and play Monopoly? Not that it happens with any great frequency, but each time it's horrible: to see another dead predator pretending to be human, a raw visage of bloody wantonness, a mirror of terror and loneliness -we practically run from each other. There's not going to be any banquet, no "Vampire Circus," no ghastly coven to convene. Just a vivid reminder that we are death-addled, mad to consume what we once were and can never be again. Sometimes, we drink to forget. Just like all of you.

My third vampire. The one who made me the man I am today. Him. *Him.* Him, I went looking for. Through my own research, trial and error, and sifting through the half-truths, outright lies, and contradictory lore within the chat group, I ultimately achieved victory. That chat group. What is it about goths that is ultimately so disappointing? We certainly have a lot in common in terms of music taste, clothing, and disposition. I assign to them, however, a lack of commitment, whatever that is. Such poseurs. They would post about impending assignations, drop broad hints that they'd found "the One" -or more darkly romantic, that "the One" had found them, that they had been selected, chosen, et cetera, always with an impending midnight meeting at an undisclosed location. Hints of historic cemeteries and then sudden silence. No more posts. This happened with enough frequency that I was able to locate variations of screen names and discern stylistic similarities in Myspace rants, which led me to discover that the lot were still working their shifts at Publix in Florida or studying for their MFA at Wellesley or Smith. Always, they would eventually reappear in the chat group, with a new screen name, displaying wonder and novice curiosity. I would comment, "Welcome back."

Still, the Russians, whenever they stopped complaining, would *dish*. It was from their lot that I learned that not only did the vampire prefer a subterranean habitat, but they also favored underground travel. Their fear of sunlight translated to a fear of the surface. While New York is a desiccated spiderweb of subway stations and tunnels, the majority of the outer borough lines run above ground. Manhattan offers a deep network of forgotten or underutilized passageways and abandoned substations. Leftover tunnels from prohibition connect restaurant and hotel basements to this dark maze. That was my "ah-ha" moment. Linking these buried dots, I knew that several of the older gay bars were all run by the mafia in the then-not-too-distant past. And not just bars; at that time, there were also saunas and bathhouses. One, in the East Village, The Palaver, was still open. This was the most sordid of the lot. Significantly, it was a basement club, a former speakeasy, and it soon became my preferred haunt.

Around the corner from the Boiler Room, The Palaver was considered the last stop for the drugged and horny, ancient cocksuckers, as well as those shambling men who likely didn't have a home to go to, but drank their public assistance checks, sold plasma, and casually shoplifted while waiting for either the dive bars or soup kitchens to open. Those sad souls slept in the old movie theater seats that lined the walls of The Palaver. The only light there emanated from the flickering blue Budweiser sign behind the ghostly bar, always untended -they'd long ago lost their liquor license as well as any pretense that they were an establishment serving anything other than base sexual satiation, as well as an unhygienic station for heroin users to shoot up, nod off, and luxuriate in their cerulean dreams.

I would have a few drinks at the Boiler Room before sauntering over. Cash only, no coat check. A warren of doorless rooms and a layout that was purposefully difficult to memorize. The haze from cigarette smoke sculptured a grey curvature to the main chamber, painting a doomy cathedral of degenerate lust. I didn't want to show up too drunk or too horny, and not reconnoiter but hook up with one of the straggly hustlers with damp pubes that frequented the joint, but also not too sober that being there made me question my commitment to this lifelong quest.

I'd been frequenting The Palaver for months by then, and knew that I had found a veritable feeding ground: the cigarette-strewn floors were actually earthen and would soak up any spilled blood. Several of the furthest walls were mere plywood, easily concealing hidden tunnels. After all, multiple subway lines were only blocks away in either direction. The proof, however, came one chilly dawn. I had stumbled out of The Palaver, having spent my rent money on a gamey hustler in black jeans. Shirtless in January, he needed the cash more than I did. I lit my last cigarette as a quiet ambulance slid down the street and stopped before the nondescript entrance. Two skeletal medics with matching mullets and bad posture crept out and retrieved a stretcher as the door swung back open. All of the more established nightclubs were known to discreetly hire private ambulances to ferry away the recently overdosed, to better hide rampant drug use from the cops, nervous landlords, and the ravenous press. But these guys were in no hurry. I intuited that no one had called them. This was a regular stop. Like sanitation workers, they were here to pick up the trash.

I finished my cigarette and flicked the butt into the street. The medics emerged, sheeted body between them. As the silent ambulance pulled away, that shirtless hustler, hands shoved deep into his pockets, shot me his most winning and desperate smile from across the street. I ignored him; I had finally tapped the right vein -struck a vital artery, one where the already forgotten regularly converged to be consumed and discarded.

My first vampire. I was twelve in the emergency room. How he shimmered, a white shadow on the periphery as the hospital staff converged above me. He was among them but separate, benign but lethal, seen but unseen. He was that powerful. That *ancient*. Everyone in his presence was mesmerized, deferring to him, obeying him, and forgetting him. This memory is centrifugal to my life; he had been making the rounds at hospitals since the concept of a hospital had come into existence. Hovering there, forever a respected doctor, but no one knew his name or could describe his appearance, offering sage diagnoses that were immediately accepted. He was tall, ghostly pale (of course); ever-alert eyes twinkled like dark rubies, and his smile revealed teeth that could rend metal.

How he smiled.

He grinned at me over the shoulders of the nurses checking my vitals while chatting amongst themselves. I was bloodied and bruised from the car accident. Coughing, struggling under the intense light above, panicked from so many people nonchalantly crowding around me, I saw this lingering shape for seconds only, but I knew what he was. I knew and he knew that I knew. My young mind decoded that red smile as he peeled away, toward a less hardy sacrifice: *Maybe next time.*

Just as Deadheads circle concert venues like tie-dyed vultures looking for their "miracle ticket" and uninfected gay men weirdly romanticizing HIV seek infection and are called "bug chasers," so too do wannabe vampiric victims have a name for that which they seek: "bestowal." "I so want to be bestowed." "Desperately seeking bestowal." "Looking to get bestowed this weekend, anyone have a master to share?" - Frequent online posts, desperate jests, or pleas; it doesn't matter. "Craving the life crimson" is always a favorite. Honestly, fantasies of death are *the* most flamboyant way to stay alive. Late at night, you would see silent internet surfers enter the chat group but never comment. Everyone assumed these were vampires, or chat group members with fake profiles looking to deceive or upstage online rivals. I always felt that the screennames gave it away: Nghtg1ft, Mercy4u69, obvious fakes; the nondescript, the culturally unaware 77777h, or MALAGA. Maybe they were there to feed, to set up private assignations in the message feature. Or they were just hovering. Like bats. Curious about what we said about them, how we think. Why wouldn't the living dead troll the dead living?

It wasn't that long after I spied the ambulance that I was able to corner a vampire at The Palaver. I knew I would have the upper hand if I could catch one right after it had fed. I just knew that that night was going to be *the* night. I cabbed it from the Roxy and arrived late. Men were fucking or sucking in every corner. Though still winter, the subterranean heat was carnal. I could smell Amyl Nitrite, sweat, fecund lust, bad breath, and something dank and dangerous underneath it all: my vampire. I wound my way through the labyrinth, toward the farthest corner, to find him feasting on an unconscious junky.

The vampire resembled a businessman, an office worker who lived upstate and removed his wedding ring as he entered a Times Square hooker bar. Closer inspection: the suit jacket was threadbare, covering a shirt deeply stained, and his shoes didn't match. Sated and drugged, having drained a likely heroin addict, he stared at me unblinking as I stepped into the doorless hovel. The addict had wilted in his arms. Tiny rivulets of blood leaked from his emaciated neck. The vampire's long fingers curled and uncurled as I approached. His stench was overpowering. Keeping the cooling corpse between us, I stroked my neck with one hand to clarify that I was offering myself to him; with the other hand, I grasped his crotch. The Russians claimed that male vampires become engorged as they feed, and that this is from where you can draw the gift of immortality (for female vampires, veiny breasts fill with black blood). Stoned, giddy over his luck at having drained one hapless victim only to have another willing source of sustenance appear, he dove toward my neck as I bent to his crotch; the stench defied description. I retched, fumbling at the zipper, fearful I would lose consciousness and then my life. But his large penis flopped out. As it engorged, the foreskin revealed likely decades of oily, granulated grime. I forced myself to again not vomit as his fangs scratched at the back of my neck. His cock in my mouth, the cooling corpse of the now-dead junky between us, the vampire was unable to gain sufficient traction as I sucked on his surprisingly strong erection. The heroin enriched blood must have fully saturated his system by then, as his body went slack. His cock tasted like what I imagine the lining of a coffin would taste like, if you were to teethe on the pink satin that had fully absorbed the liquified remains of whichever body had decomposed within its interred confines. He came. He shot globular death into my mouth and down my constricting throat. I died and was immediately reborn, choking on the black cement of his congealing, lifeless semen, sealing my fate.

I actually felt my heart stop.

All these years, I could hear it but didn't realize it. Like someone rhythmically knocking on an unseen door for so long, for three decades to be exact, that it wasn't until the invisible person had left that the absence of pulsing noise became startlingly omnipresent. The now-missing but quite persistent force would have been my departed soul. I gasped and heaved, and the vampire giggled and tucked his deflating dick back into his soiled pants. He didn't look at me as he kicked at the corpse on the ground, trying to determine if there was another drop of blood in there to still be had. I didn't care about him. I didn't care about myself. My only thought was of the chorus of hearts I could now hear singing throughout the extended maze.

The thirst was overwhelming.

The Palaver was closed down by the city a few years later.

All of the massive dance clubs shuttered—the one human who looked the most vampiric, Mayor Guliani, was responsible. In a budgetary fight with the Governor, he also pulled city funding from the subway system, further condemning it to its current downward spiral, marked by non-existent cleanliness and disintegrating reliability. Fine by me. I rarely take the subway. The allure of the tunnels, the earthen pull, the aphrodisiac of all those dead rats rotting on the tracks - it's a battle to resist, but if I were to hunt underground, I would be forever lost. The war our kind fights is not with the sun but with the intoxicating darkness. Down there, we lose our minds, grow feral, and I like my rent-controlled apartment; I like that I have an empty refrigerator. A white crypt, the hum of which reminds me that I used to be alive and need to maintain that appearance to better move among my livestock.

The thirst was overwhelming, but I had a plan. First thing I did was kill Reverend Rick and drink his blood. I knew he lived alone, I knew he'd let me in, I knew no one would miss a drug dealer. Importantly, I knew he kept his cash in a battered tacklebox, and that large amount of big bills set me on the right path. I also needed to see how long I could go between feedings. Something about that first vampire from my youth told me that there were unseen parameters, the Russians were on to something, but I had to test it. Now a nocturnal being, I was able to maintain a modicum of self-control as long as I didn't spend too much time below. The less said about my vampiric brothers and sisters who take to the ground and what becomes of them, the better. Manhattan has twenty-one bridges, and I feed on their midnight suicides. The night air does me good. It's nice to see the stars.

I persist. I don't go online anymore, though I have spied some of my former chat group members across the dance floor. Aging goths swathed in black crinoline. The Palaver has reopened as a speakeasy, and I DJ there. I'm really good at whipping up the crowd. The changes in my hearing have made me more attuned to what motivates the body, the sounds that get hearts beating—music to *my* ears.

I also like to take a young man home now and again (no one jumps off bridges when it rains or on really cold nights. Go figure). So, I pluck someone from the dancefloor. Someone new to the city. Someone alive to the possibilities of the night, to every possibility but what I have to offer. Back at my place, I ask them to disrobe while I play a record. I put them at ease by talking about the singer, by dissecting the song. In bed, my fingers trace every available vein. I savor the slow caress, the shivers I can entice from the body beneath me. When it's time to take that singular bite, I always pause and stand before them naked. I want them to see me, all of me, as I then walk across the room to the record player. Once the needle hits black vinyl, I smile that red smile at them, and then they know. They always know that this is their last night. The relief that washes over their faces - faces as inviting as any cathedral ceiling, overflowing with the ecstasy of prayer.

I always play my favorite song.

A Seppuku of Centerfolds

The striking, Borgesian death of Wren Cartwright is *the* forgotten story of East Village lore. Precisely because the neighborhood has experienced seismic tumult, from the crack epidemic to the AIDS crisis to rapid gentrification, it has left few witnesses to such an eccentric lifestyle and its improbable end. Thus, separating reality from anecdote is that much more difficult.

While alive, Wren Cartwright was but one among a veritable platoon of tatterdemalion book scouts who threaded the New York City subway systems, slouching subterranean travelers who emerged into the light of day only to plunge into musty, outer-borough second-hand stores, canvasing estate sales upstate for first editions or bundles of Civil War letters that had, until then, been rotting in attics. Chelsea flea markets were frequent battlegrounds as this horde of hustlers possessed sharp elbows and shrewd, encyclopedic knowledge of literary arcana. They were known to screech at one another if they happened to reach for a fine, embossed copy of *Treasure Island* in unison. Auction houses, book collectors, and the less-esteemed bookstores of the Upper East Side all purchased their wares (some shopkeepers met these grubby shades at the back door, where they were paid for their pickings off the books and in cash). They were always men, mostly middle-aged or wizened, be-speckled bachelors on the march, daily circling New York City, moving just enough books to survive at a subsistent level. Most wore a laminated copy of their independent retailer's license on a thread around their neck to silently signal to timid clerks that they didn't have to pay sales tax. All were on the hunt for that elusive white whale in book form to lift them from poverty. That veritable *Moby Dick* would surface on the horizon during blazing sunsets of rent-fueled desperation at the end of every month—a first edition Fitzgerald that, at a glance, looked to be signed by the infamous alcoholic, only it was the scribbled name of the book's previous owner. With an exhausted sigh, the volume was slung onto the counter for purchase as the fog of false hope swirled anew.

Except for Wren Cartwright. He miraculously scored.

As the story goes, told and retold among scouts, collectors, and retailers, one humid July afternoon, he found himself at a Brooklyn Heights church rummage sale. There, within a box of old newspapers and coverless paperbacks secreted within a battered, stained, and nearly unsalable copy of *Leaves of Grass* was a cache of yellowed letters from a young Bram Stoker to the master himself. They nearly slid out and onto the dirty gray sidewalk. Words unread for a century. Even better, drafts of Whitman's appreciative replies were tucked in as well. Scribbles of his poetry reached for the margins. Wren clutched the parcel to his heaving chest with one hand while thrusting exact change at the volunteer salesperson, lest they, in breaking a dollar bill, had time to inspect the item, declare it a treasure reserved for the ecclesiastical coffers, and set it aside as no longer for sale. He stuffed the receipt into his greasy billfold and fled down into the subway. These feral booksellers were a shrewd bunch, and Wren knew that the letters were going to lift him out of poverty like bat wings. For at that moment, the revival of *Dracula* ruled Broadway. The black etchings of Edward Gorey's poster for the play were plastered all over town. As his discovery was just a few years after the Stonewall riot, gay culture was on the rise, and as such, letters of this nature were quite collectible. Wren's whale had surfaced in a perfect confluence of trend, popular culture, and exclusivity. The faded bookplate declared the owner of this volume to have been the sexton of the very church where Cartwright had made the purchase. Whitman had famously lived in the area, so provenance was not a problem. He knew not to take the letters to the bookstores; they would preemptively dismiss his find, outright devalue it, and begrudgingly offer a pittance, selling the letters in the window at a criminally high markup. No, treasure such as this was destined for an international seller, likely for auction to the highest bidder. Bypassing Manhattan's big-name auction houses and their byzantine approval processes, he shakily made the rare long-distance call to a London firm that dealt only in books and manuscripts, and they immediately set an appointment for their New York representative to inspect the letters. In short order, the sale was made to an anonymous collector with a standing order to pay top dollar for items relating to a short list of favored authors. The buyer went public after the sale with the intent of gifting some of the letters to Trinity College Dublin. Biographers for both writers cawed to the press that this was the literary discovery of the decade. Within a fortnight of his find, a large amount of money was wallowing in Wren Cartwright's bank account. And with this, some of his habits began to change: not his dress, he still took the subway, he still ate miserly in out-of-the-way diners; though he continued to move books around town, for the first time in his mostly unrecorded life, Wren began to acquire for taste, not profit.

While little is known of Cartwright before his windfall, more is known about the years leading up to his dramatic demise. Public records offer up a birth in Delaware, an unfinished degree in English Literature from Stetson University in Florida (it's speculated that he left as a result of a campus-wide purge of homosexual students and staff. There's no evidence for this except the explicit timing of his hasty move north). Tax returns show a variety of low-paying clerking jobs until his obsessive love of literature eventually translated into a peripatetic existence of selling books while living in a variety of SROs up and down the fringes of Manhattan. It's worth noting that the majority of his early residences were always within walking distance of major gay cruising spots on the city's Westside, though any connection is purely conjecture. As far as we know, Cartwright left no journals and lived a friendless life outside of his connections to the book trade. He disowned or was disowned by his family (they refused to collect his corpse, which was cremated and buried on Hart Island, a potter's field off the Bronx, so overfed with the bodies of New York City's forgotten that skulls roll ashore on Orchard Beach after strong storms). His drift into a hermitic existence is hard to trace, though money from the Stoker-Whitman sale fueled an unstated resolve. He immediately moved to a large, ground-floor studio in the East Village at a time when it was a cheap and dangerous neighborhood. The Bowery was blighted, muggings common. Since he could have afforded safer, more luxurious housing, in hindsight, it is tempting to surmise that he chose this apartment neither for thrift nor location, but the noteworthy rarity that his front door both opened to the street and was equipped with a mail slot.

There are many different types of bibliomanias. Beyond the typical affinity for genre, there are literary manias that, oddly, have gone unrecorded. At the time, Wren Cartwright's death received little notice outside a curt, riddle-like headline in the August 5th, 1998 edition of *The New York Post*: *Porn Addict Chokes To Death on Smut*. His peculiar story has gained more attention in recent years as hoarding, the compulsive collecting of things, has moved from an obscure concern among social workers and into the public sphere via reality shows and social media. While the tapestry of New York City is stained with countless lonely deaths, none have ever been as articulate or as unusual as Wren Cartwright's suicide.

With the Stoker-Whitman sale, his focus shifted entirely onto gay erotica and pornography. The mass of gay pulp produced during prior decades was, at that time, dismissed and grossly underappreciated. These steamy sex romps from the fifties and sixties were discarded as more emboldened, celebratory gay pornography followed the sexual revolution. Cartwright not only purchased every available copy of gay pulp that he could get his hands on—he also acquired large quantities of Bob Mizer's pictorial magazines and any and all lewd apocrypha. Bookseller and original member of New York City's Gay Men's Chorus, Ben McFall, reports that his reputation among the other booksellers was someone who paid well and in cash for any and all gay material. "I also saw him at the bars, drinking alone, always reading, never socializing. I never saw him at the baths. Most of the book scouts were straight, so I expected he'd have been pleased to see a familiar face, but he never made small talk." Similarly, Glenway Wescott biographer Jerry Rosco, a longtime resident of the East Village, knew Cartwright by sight. "He was just one of those characters you saw around town, always lugging a bag of books with him. I heard he got banned from *The Oscar Wilde Bookshop* for haranguing a customer who bought the last copy of some porno mag he lusted after." Cartwright also subscribed to every gay publication of a sexual nature. Among his known magazine and chapbook subscriptions, from the popular to the obscure (this is far from an exhaustive list), were *Backroom Tales, Black Inches, Blueboy, Bound and Gagged, Cruisers, Drum, Drummer, Freshmen, GUY, Guzzler Magazine, Honcho, International Barracks, Latin Inches, Male Nudist Review, Mandate, Mister, The Naked Male, Playguy, Ranch Hands, Raw Quarterly, Samson, Stepson Quarterly, Straight To Hell, Urge* and *Vulcan*.

He is known to have quarreled with *Straight to Hell* editor and fellow curmudgeon Boyd McDonald. Cartwright accused McDonald of withholding several early issues of STH simply to spite him. While McDonald was known to play or trick or two, he was also famously cash-strapped and would have benefited from Cartwright's largess, so it's likely a minor dust-up in some Times Square porn store has transmogrified into legend. It's an interesting juxtaposition: Cartwright, as the consummate consumer, frequented the same haunts as editor Boyd McDonald and science fiction and fantasy author Samuel R. Delaney, writers who explicitly recorded the erotic adventures Wren coveted, and was in turn consumed by a sexual Ouroboros of gluttony. One can't help but think that, though Delaney and McDonald were the risk-takers, desire triumphs obsession, as at least desire can be *spent*. With obsession, accumulation occurs until somewhere a dam breaks, either psychically or otherwise.

From the limited information we can gain from the police report, there was no furniture in Wren's apartment, with the exception of a spent mattress on the floor. Every inch was given over to his burgeoning library. Even the refrigerator had been removed some years prior; his corpse was described as emaciated, so at some point his collecting trapped/entombed him. His rent was paid far enough in advance to guarantee mummification before his body was discovered. So much is unknown, including whether the mailman who made the fateful delivery was aware that he or she had inadvertently caused the death of another human being. Nor was it possible to know which magazine delivered the fateful blow, enforcing a seppuku of centerfolds and tan lines down Cartwright's open mouth, choking him to death. No photographs of the scene, quickly ruled a suicide, survive. (No photographs taken of the reclusive Cartwright while he was alive have to come to light, either.) What was apparent, however, was that the abundance of books and magazines, and likely rare manuscripts and letters, was arranged in such a way as to act as gears. Each conveyance of pornographic material in anonymous brown paper wrappers during those final days set a domino process in motion. At some point, Cartwright could no longer rise from his bed. Enthroned on piles of pulp as mail was pushed through the slot, prior deliveries were propelled forward. Think of the dark architectural designs from the great eighteenth-century illustrator Piranesi come to life. The meticulousness of this paper clockwork meant that, near starvation, Wren Cartwright was able to purse his lips and receive one final delivery, extreme unction, possibly in the form of a California surfer, nude, looking over his sun-kissed shoulder, a wave about to break that never will.

The complexity of this machination cannot be overstated. The singularity of the design is overwhelming: the entire apartment and all of its contents were arranged to act as a slow-moving guillotine, his obscene library serving double duty as a deadly apparatus, a contraption the creation of which required an outré imagination and nearly fiendish planning. It's likely models were built and tested, attempts failed, plans revisited; the investment of time, the sheer determination, is unfathomable and augments Cartwright's suicide to a new form of self-expression, surpassing the mere politics of immolated monks and all their ilk.

It is now considered culturally criminal that such a vast collection of pornography, one that likely represented the entire erotic output of gay America up until his death, was unceremoniously hauled to the dump. This loss was described by poet and Assistant Professor of Creative Writing at Merrick Community College, Philip F. Clark, as "The burning of our Library of Alexander. Or more likely our Library of Bagoas, Alexander's boy-eunuch lover, for those magazines were in their own way love letters. The men pictured had the bodies we all coveted; the stories were ones we could only tell each other." Likely somewhere within the now-defunct Fresh Kills landfill, this buried museum quietly rots. Glossy buttocks, mimeographed cocks, page after page of torrid encounters, and anatomical descriptions are blindly churned to soil by innumerable insects. Was Wren Cartwright's collection a suicide note or a paean to beauty, an example of unchecked mental illness or a fanatical act of deviance: one of carnal images and lurid letters, a cut-up like no other, designed to make the ghost of William S. Burroughs stew in jealousy within his bunker, just a few blocks away? On the tenth anniversary of his death, painter and performance artist Lorenzo De Los Angeles launched a one-night art installation at the East Village experimental theater, La MaMa, symbolically recreating Wren Cartwright's moment of death. Inspired by the erotic artistry of Surrealist Hans Bellmer, works of gay pornography were connected by an intricate web of strings to a plastic skeleton being force-fed images via an elaborate series of funnels in a room created by cardboard boxes. Every time a viewer plucked at one of the strings, another image would slide into the skeleton's unhinged jaws, filling the fishbowl ensconced within its ribcage, making the viewer complicit in Cartwright's demise. Outside of De Los Angeles's moving sculpture and a passing mention in Gary Indiana's autobiography that he suspected Cartwright of swiping the original manuscript of his first novel, *Horse Crazy*, New York City's culture commentary on Cartwright's bizarre demise has been surprisingly minimal. Only singer Dean Johnson of the Velvet Mafia is known to have consistently memorialized the compulsive collector. After Wren's passing, he frequently dedicated shows to him. (Johnson's own 2007 death is shrouded in mystery.)

The methodical premeditation of such a suicide surpasses the typical diagnosis of hoarding, which is based on the fear of letting go. With Cartwright's death, we have the creation of an Egyptian tomb, replete with homoerotic hieroglyphs. The mailman was merely a servant laying the last brick, sealing the sepulcher, as it were. Or is his death a mystery we will never solve? Should we avoid reflexively painting it as a tragedy? For if his actions were a thanatological embrace of the erotic life society had tried so hard to evict him from, then Wren Cartwright can be said to have built not a tomb, but a cathedral of desire, one whose collapse he himself orchestrated, as all religions eventually implode as sacrament begets sacrifice.

Double Feature

T*he Casket Fantastic Double Feature* show is winding down. Every Halloween, until midnight, the local Avondale television station shows two classic horror movies back-to-back. The perennial host, Mr. Moonlight: the beleaguered evening news weatherman disguised in clown white and a cloud of talcum powder, dark circles under his eyes. Playing the ghoul, he delivers some truly awful puns between commercial breaks. On the couch, Brad groans and nudges Lee with his knee, hoping that the connection will last longer. When they were younger, up in Brad's tree house, while sharing a *Heavy Metal* magazine Brad had shoplifted from the Seven-Eleven on Shell Road –the one right before the turn off to the beach, their knees touched the entire time: Lee shirtless and golden brown as always, a silent eternity Brad had forever wanted to recapture.

Now, in their senior year, they were left to watch the house and manage the trick-or-treaters while their parents were out of town. It had been hours since the last coterie of kids had rang the doorbell -Brad had lurched in his makeshift mummy costume, loosely wrapped around his skinny frame, extenuated ace bandages now sagging at night's end. Lee gave his best Frankenstein, lumbering to the door, stiff-legged, green body-paint smeared across his thick chest, a borrowed blazer from his dad about to come off the shoulder. Every time Brad sees one of Lee's wide nipples, he thinks about that afternoon in the tree house, the electricity between them unspent. Would it evaporate when they both left for college after the soon-to-come summer?

Lee yawns, the empty Budweiser bottle between his legs drops onto the shag carpet. Finally old enough to buy beer, but still carded each and every time, they had shared a six-pack and smoked a joint in the backyard. The sky was a neon dark blue, blurry with clouds, and a nuisance of mosquitoes. Brad intuits that Lee is pretending to be more drunk than he is: legs spread wide, chest exposed: an invitation –but to what? On the giant Magnavox, the black and white credits roll. The last film was *Bride of Frankenstein*. The host cracks several bad jokes in quick succession, and suddenly the television is a crackle of electric snow, then goes dark. Usually, at midnight, they play the national anthem. Brad openly sighs. Another wasted evening of unspent longing and misdirected desire. He stands, thinking to give the television a whack for good measure, and surveys Lee's jock-ish form: arm across his eyes, bare chest exposed, black hair greasy and matted, full lips parted as if he were about to snore. The television flickers and brightens.

The midnight room fills with light.

Brad blinks and reaches for the remote control. He struggles to turn the television off as *Bride of Frankenstein* comes to life again. It is the scene where the Bride screams, repelled by the Monster. Except this time she stares at him, and he looks back. Brad drops the remote. Lee sits up, and the sizzle of static and blinding light envelopes him. The Bride unwinds her bandages, and in unison, as if possessed, so does Brad. When they had put on their costumes earlier, Lee had stood before the bathroom mirror in his white distended briefs while he applied his emerald make-up; the black flash of his underarm hair seemed like a precursor to all that was below –where Brad's imagination had spent many a night tossing and turning. Now Lee disrobes slowly while the twin creatures glitter on TV. Frankenstein's Monster reaches for his Bride. More bandages drop as Brad steps into Lee's arms and feels the heat from his chest, the bulge in the young man's unbuttoned jeans hard against his thigh.

31

On the television Bride kisses Monster. Brad and Lee kiss, wide-eyed, open-mouthed, hands up and down one another's ribs, breathing heavy, beery breaths of attenuated wonderment.

The television goes dark.

The tiny white dot of light in the center of the screen collapses in on itself, and the spell is broken. Mouths unclasped. Hands on each other's hips, they knew what came next: Brad had watched his best friend undress for years when they had stayed the night at each other's houses. Lee took his time after a shower, Black Sabbath trudging on the cassette player in either of their bedrooms —they both listened to the same bands and were constantly trading tapes in the hall: Krokus, Judas Priest, Iron Maiden. He usually paused when putting on a fresh pair of underwear to finish whatever story he was telling, less to exclaim and more to allow Brad time to examine his body, which had developed sooner than the other boys in his class. Brad was fascinated by the black tangle of pubic hair that converged over his friend's tumescent cock and each time had tried not to stare.

Tonight, Halloween, he let his fingers undo Lee's jeans to reach in and free his hot erection. Lee knew to stand back and let his friend discover what had previously been just out of reach —his hands grasp and pull at his jeans, and soon he is naked, save white tube socks and a smear of remaining green body paint. The Florida air is unusually humid for October. Brad on his knees, bandages a tatter, his sallow chest panting, filled with fear and longing -knowing that the engorged cock before him belongs in his mouth. Lee deliberately grunts like the Frankenstein Monster and breaks the tension: Brad smiles up at him, they always crack each other up —he sticks out his tongue. With his wide thumb, Lee pushes his thick, sweaty dick between his best friend's parted lips. Brad buys himself some time by kissing the flanged ridge of Lee's pulsing cock —wondering if taking it in his mouth would give them both one night of pleasure while ending years of friendship. The hand gripping the back of his head was one of reassurance, not pressure, and he knows that his service will be rewarded with a deeper, naked friendship of discovery and joy. He takes the considerable cock to the root and sucks slowly, to signal that his is a knowing surrender: not one of lust but trust. Brad pulls his underwear down and rubs the pre-come previously coating the head of his cock up and down his shaft while Lee's eyes roll back in his head. Brad steadies himself on Lee's bony feet and keeps as much flesh in his mouth as possible, gulping his sex, dazed by the salty effluence easily issuing forth. They both shake with ecstasy. Neither can contain themselves –this force has been building for years. Both explode. Lee's searing come fills Brad's mouth as his own pent-up fluid leaks onto the carpet between his red, now-chafed knees. The young men exhale. Brad collapses onto the floor, spent, dazed. Lee pulls off his socks, knowing that they are far from done.

The television blooms back to life. The face of Frankenstein's Monster fills the flashing ocher screen in its entirety, his mouth open, about to either exclaim a command or express some suppressed craving, but no sound comes forth: he is alive with lightning on a night without end.

Mother of All Bats

A wing that spread slowly, an eclipse blacking out the moon. The sleeping cattle below shifted warily on the arid ground as a piercing darkness penetrated their dreams.

Then the other wing unfurled, shaking off a long slumber, covering the nearby mountaintop, alerting their enclosure of pine that a great hunger had at last awakened. The Mother of all Bats knew to shift slowly, lest the beating of her wings roil the landscape: flatten trees, upend streams, scatter the animals from which she needed to feed. As an arrow falls, so she parted the night and snatched a cow from the field with a stealth and speed that rendered the animal in her jaws unconscious. She supped far above the clouds, where the circumference of the earth was visible, the bleeding ochre of dawn present. She dropped the drained corpse from such a height that the force of the winds rendered it into a fine, red mist. Then she went off -off to sleep, coasting above the world, a shadow to satellites, a vision to shaman, a God to the depraved, a warning to us all.

The Mother of all Bats was no such thing. She was peerless, a primeval animal from a time when men were soundless, shaped differently, moved as if spat out from pits of hot clay that percolated in lifeless pools of spiny rock covered in silver dust. Unlike her fellow bats that clung to cliffs and shrubbery and harried lumbering mammals, she continued to grow and refused to die. After several eons, this made her the largest living creature to scour the planet, succor to a black constellation of minuscule bats who lived entire generations within the protection of her expansive wings, though a reflexive sneeze on her part could kill thousands nestled in membranous folds. One dusk, as she scoured the land for a particularly large animal that she had long savored, Mother (let's call her mother) realized that she had feasted the species into extinction. So, she took to the clouds and ate ether, and began to consider her service to the rapidly shrinking world below. This new consciousness allowed her to arrest her growth and control her hunger. She realized she was alone. As she skirted the seas, Mother sensed large, wingless creatures rollicking below, animals filled with song caring for calves. Jealousy raked her body, and for the first time in several hundred years, she fed with abandon, painting a mountain red with the blood of giant horses. She had no mate, so she willed it so: dislodging one of her fangs, she planted the raw, red bone in the center of one of the fern-rung bogs that the men, who now painted their flesh and coveted fire, slipped the bodies of their dead into, as if providing a passage to another world. Her giant, icy tooth sank, and she despaired. As Mother was about to take flight again, the bog hissed and oozed a threatening heat. The tooth arose slick, different, embryonic. It fused to the surface, pulsing with molten warmth. The Mother of all Bats was riven with new emotion and thoughts and irrational fears: should she stay beside the earthen fetus, but what if she stayed so long that she forgot how to fly? What if she left to feed, and one of the wide gray crocodiles that haunted the nearby rivers ate her only child? She then heard its heartbeat for the first time and recognized the rhythm of the night song that she sang to herself, and she was calm again.

Her child was born appropriately at night, without eyes, a shaking, wet, obsidian thing, all mouth and teeth. Suckling the beast above the clouds, Mother felt content and challenged:

this living thing against her breast was an echo of her own soul, but its relentless feeding meant she needed to consume more herself, so she plucked fat gray sloths from a beautiful forested island. The creatures had never been hunted before. The pestilence of mankind had yet to discover this land, and after depopulating the island of its sacrificial flesh, she ruminated that she herself had left it alone to preserve its unique tranquility. Her child grew into a spirited daughter, shadowing her in flight, in hunting, sharing everything with her except the night song, which allowed Mother to feel the earth, the shape of mountains, and know how far to fly. Maybe this song comes later, as the daughter matures, she thought. As her child grew, she was petulantly at her mother's breast, demanding milk when above the clouds and the blood of every beast below. Exasperated, Mother had observed aggressive behavior in the offspring of other creatures, but never such an unending thirst, with one exception.

Is this what it means to be immortal? She thought.

Long ago, when she circled the earth looking for others of her kind, she watched from above as a storm of locusts swept across vast fields in a frenzy of senseless plunder. She thought of the long songs spun by the shadowy family of forms within the oceans and felt that not all was right with her daughter. Perhaps it was because her child did not yet possess eyes to take census of what lives, or the song of the night to know the shape of the world, to feel its limits, to best apprehend her own hunger. The Mother of all Bats tried to coax song from her child, but the beast just beat her head on the rocks or drooled with incomprehension. While this insatiable nursling slumbered against her breast as they sailed far above, Mother nuzzled her, instinctively inspecting for parasites. With the long, lone clawed appendage at the cusp of her wing, she picked at the wet seal of the wizened pits where the infant's eyes should be. She found a mad array of seething baby teeth nestled within the sockets, two mouths about to blossom on either side of her coal-colored snout. Mother's heart withered. Borne from the pointed tooth of lonesome desire, she had given birth to something that was perpetual craving; she understood that it would eventually grow larger than her, consuming her to envelope the world with furious wings. Mother sailed on. She knew of a place from her earlier travels where all the anger of the earth smoldered and boiled over into a hot, red lake. She forced a tired breast into the gaping mouth of her sleeping babe, and willed warm milk to flood its mouth so the child would be satiated, know she was loved, not feel the temperature rise as they closed in over the broken, seeping mountain -then the shock of being decoupled; the cry, her first attempt at night song! As she plummeted, the failed flapping ignited her wings, and then she was consumed. The meaty smoke plume unwound across the horizon. No matter how far Mother flew, it hung there like the thick incense of her sorrow.

Bereft, alone, she withdrew from the world. There were still caverns big enough to contain her. She emerged every so often to stretch her mile-long wings, to feel the wind, to feed. She is far from content when she awakens, however, as she hears less song from the now polluted oceans. What she does discern is degraded; the long aquatic soliloquies are gone, replaced by messages of survival and mourning. The Mother of all Bats sees that man has clawed away much of the earth, erecting unnatural barriers while hording animals in ways shocking and cruel. Their towers and the multitude of objects launched into the air infest the atmosphere and diffuse her night song. She understands that there might not be a place for her here much longer. (She had long been curious about the promising quietude of the moon.)

Once again, she glides above everything, resolute. Before she leaves, she will spit out thousands upon thousands of sharp teeth across the globe—one unquenchable brood to consume another.

A Surprise in Every Box

"The undeclared yet protracted 'cereal wars" heated up with the advent of Saturday morning cartoons. Bland, out-of-date packaging couldn't compete with the techno-color critters crawling out of televisions to settle in the laps of hypnotized pre-teens. Forget licensing; since the meteoric rise of the rock band KISS, every brand with a shot at the youth market was a fully realized force: figurines, board games, snacks, even band aids, flooded department store aisles. The good people at Kernel Incorporated took their cue from the fast food giants and charged their advertizing department with creating a bevy of memorable, enticing, lawsuit-proof characters to competitively sell cereal."

—*What's For Breakfast, America? The History of Cereal, A Billion Dollar A Year Industry*, Franklin Shorthorn, 1998.

The red lanterns of the twisted alley somewhere in the heart of Kyoto's Gion-district glowed like candied cherries. The Kernel sales team stumbled after their Japanese hosts. That last round of sake had done more than loosen tongues and ties and strengthen professional relationships. Everyone was drunk. Rod Carver had dreamed of writing comic books since he discovered a stack of battered and torn issues featuring the exploits of World War II hero, The Spirit of Broadway, whose black cape extended in every direction to ensnare Nazi spies and obscure the windows of citizens who forgot to observe curfew. He still had every tattered issue, packed away with his baseball cards in the top of the closet. Though he wasn't part of the sales team assembled to break through in the Asia market, he was included because he had been to Japan while in the service -he protested that he drank his way through leave, barely recalled a scant ten words of Japanese, but was sent anyway to shake him out of his malaise. Though popular with his younger colleagues, none of his pitches had taken hold. He'd been relegated to simple drafting assignments as recently hired staff introduced successful new brands. This trip was a reward for time served and meant to put him on notice that he needed to come up with something *soon*. Their Japanese hosts seemed to hold their liquor better. The main host, Yokio, stood before the entrance of a yakitori joint and held the curtain open for his comrades. Rod waved and smiled. He wanted a break from the incessant smoking of the Japanese and the constant questions his colleagues teasingly lobbed at him, treating him as if he were an expert on all things Japan, no matter how inane –he played along, making up ridiculous answers, but was now counting the days until the trip came to an end. He stepped back down the alley and ducked into a tiny shop filled with lacquerware. The young woman tending the shop bowed deeply as he entered.

Every black and vermilion object was displayed perfectly on simple cedar boards. The simplicity of design and the orderliness of the shop set him at ease. Time stopped. Their hosts had explained that many of these shops were three and four hundred years old –older than the American Dream that The Spirit of Broadway had righteously defended! Yokio, having studied at Amherst, spoke perfect English, and both were delighted to discover a shared appreciation for comic books. However, Rod couldn't quite muster the guts to ask how Yokio felt about his countrymen being the villains in so many of the titles they shared an obsession over. He reached for a particularly beautiful bowl and realized how unsteady the alcohol had made him. Embarrassed, he steeled himself and moved to the other side of the shop. A dark corner held a clutch of antiques. An elegant onyx-colored jewelry box was open; it contained miniature marvels that he had to squint to make out. His back to the shopkeeper, he bent over the box: each object appeared to be a polished carving, a tiny enticing totem, each a different color of stone. He was drawn to a round of milky, orange quartz. At a distance, it would have looked like a common pebble, but he held it up to his eyes and could discern a face both joyous and malevolent, something like a jack-o'-lantern. The stone was both warm and heavy in his palm. An image of the trickster fox, like a flame shimmering in a field of snow, then ancient watchers in the woods, flashed through his mind, and he smiled drunkenly as inspiration struck. Yokio called to him from the doorway. Rod quickly turned, absently pocketed his new lucky charm as he rushed out, excited to rejoin his colleagues and secretly toast to the latest ideas percolating in his skull. He couldn't wait to get back to his cramped hotel room and start sketching.

"In 1978, one of the odder choices on the American breakfast table was Pumpykins, a Halloween-themed cereal. Wildly popular with children due to a series of episodic cartoon commercials, Pumpykins was short-lived, its demise long-rumored to be related somehow to the urban myth of razors secreted within apples given out at Halloween, that something similarly malevolent lurked in the box, causing parents to reflexively shun the product. However, Kernel Inc. maintains that profits of Pumpykins were negated by the increasingly expense cartoons, and was thus deemed unviable. Pulled en masse from the market, its prizes are now highly valued and exceedingly rare. The central orange plastic creature of Pumpykins, depicted as a rolling anthropomorphic vegetable in the now vintage advertisements, is among one of the most sought after and hard to find figurines of that era."

—*Pop Culture Collectibles Price Guide: Revised Edition*, Mary Shears, 1999.

The lush aquamarine shag carpet was the ocean Mikey sprinkled LEGO across – tiny, sharp bricks his father was forever stepping on barefoot, eliciting cries of pain. LEGO were assembled into crashed spaceships. A variety of action figures from across a motley assortment of movies and TV shows battled, joined forces, and conspired against each other on the water planet of Mikey's envisioning. The large wood-paneled Magnavox television was the permanent sun. All play stopped at exactly 9 AM for *The World Guardians Power Hour*, as his favorite heroes fought their foes. *Space Ark*, which followed, was a live-action series that only interested him somewhat, although each episode featured a new alien life form, which was worth something. His favorite, though, second to the giant toy robots his dad had brought him back from a business trip to Japan, was the Pumpykins commercials, featuring the laughing, rolling, and bouncing pumpkin, Gourdy, and his friends Witchee and Hector Specter, as they quested to escape the Forest of Evil. He marveled that his father was the creator of these wonders, and often sat silently in his lap while he sketched out stories. To Mikey, it was as if he were watching new myths unravel across the giant pad of drawing paper. He wanted badly to suggest stories, to finally let the silent but so very helpful Hector Specter talk back to the funny but bossy Witchee, but every time he tried to say something, the idea, half-formed, stuck in his throat, and he'd fidget. His father would sigh, "Daddy's working," and banish him to the living room.

Mikey was as proud as a five-year-old could be. He not only demanded Pumpykins for breakfast every morning, much to his mother's consternation, but it was his preferred snack as well. Mikey meticulously kept the empty boxes as well, as the back of the box featured panels of a continuous comic book story that elaborated on the antics within the cartoon commercials.

The cereal itself was nondescript and of questionable nutritional value. What delighted Mikey were the marshmallow figures, the wispy witches, the sugary little ghosts, and the large smiling pumpkins. As the pumpkins were weightier, they ended up congregating at the bottom of the cereal box. Exhibiting Olympic self-control, Mikey would deliberately not shake and sift them out, so when he was near the end of the box, he was able to peer inside and find a delightful menagerie grinning back at him. Then he would eat them by the fistful.

Rod Carver once again pushed the poorly fitting safety helmet up and out of his eyes. As he toured the factory, his sense of accomplishment was renewed. The workers in white coveralls were mass-producing *his* creation, *his* confectionery army that had surged through the television screen and onto kitchen tables across the country – earning him a raise, much praise, and the subsequent pressure to grow and expand a successful product line. Pumpykins was the number one selling cereal in the nation, the idea of making commercials mini-episodes considered genius across Wall Street boardrooms. The company had flown him first class to the Wisconsin factory to view the fortified fruits of his labor, as well as meet with the candy division. Halloween was six months out, and there was barely enough time to expand the product into new markets; the paper sketches of plastic masks and candy wrappers slithered against a well-thumbed issue of *Playboy*, along with reams of unread memos stuffed inside his worn brown leather satchel.

The tour guide pointed out the gigantic machine that pumped out Pumpykins treats. An unwieldy mechanical nozzle, much like a wizened elephant's trunk, was manipulated by a woman in greasy goggles to produce dollops of orange goo – an identical woman further down the line pressed smiles into them, and from there they swirled downward into open, waiting cereal boxes. Rod found this particular process slightly hypnotic; he stuck his hand in his pocket and reflexively rubbed the little totem he'd picked up in the Gion that drunken night. Throughout this fevered journey, from the hotel room where he stayed up all night doing character design, even story-boarding the rough draft of the initial cartoon commercial, to the airplane ride home where he switched seats and borrowed one of the stewardess' lipsticks to color in the final details, he'd felt on fire, more sure of himself than ever before, and whenever his determination flagged, a touch of the totem renewed his focus.

His tour guide excused himself as a group of businessmen approached. Guilt once again fluttered within Rod's stomach –he'd meant to figure out how to get a check off to that little shop back in Japan –he'd never shoplifted before in his life, but the logistics, assessing the value, his mind drifted at the complexity of it all. He took the small thing out of his pocket and examined it in the dull glare of the factory lights— the slight polish and mild inconsistencies of its surface seemingly altered its expression in different lights; often, he thought, in mimicry of his moods. Now the black slash of paint that made up its mouth looked, for the very first time since it came into his possession, like an outright sneer. As if his transgression were obvious to all. If that wasn't off-putting enough, a loud and familiar "Rod!" burst out across the factory floor. He turned and was doubly shocked: it was Yokio, marching toward him with a roll of blueprints in one hand, wearing the same safety helmet as Rod, but his fit smartly, as if he were a captain of industry and everyone around him was a bit player. Rod's guilt over the stolen stone intensified into panic –Yokio rushed in with hand proudly extended (back in Japan, he'd actually had Rod practice shaking hands with him at a baseball game one afternoon). Rod, suitcase in his other hand, fumbled as he tried to pocket his prized talisman, but it fell onto the conveyor belt below.

There was nothing he could do.

They vigorously shook hands, and then Rod stepped back to offer him a polite and proper bow, which gave him the chance to discreetly peer backward and watch as a mass of the orange treats bubbled at the mouth of the funnel. The grinding wheels and pulleys of the conveyor belt sputtered, and the entire contraption froze, pulling a bewildered Rod out of his bow. Everyone looked around for a second, and then the machine burst back to life. The marshmallows plopped into their attendant cereal boxes, which were in turn mechanically sealed shut.

"Pottery from the late Jomon period in prehistoric Japan demonstrates a further reduction in the size of totems as well as refinement in design. Those found at burial sites in the Kyushu region are possible wards against ancient demons particular to the Hyakki Yagyō, an annual parade of goblins and ghouls that spirit away any poor soul who happens to witness their night of mischief."

—*Islands of Ice and Fire: Japan Before It Was Japan*,
Jonathan Richie, 1969.

Halloween night, and the Carver family was sprawled out in the living room; the made-for-TV film *Gargoyles* was on, but the sound was turned off. Mikey had emptied the worn pillow case he'd used for trick-or-treating across the carpet. He openly marveled at his haul, a Hector Specter mask pushed up over his sweaty forehead. His mother had admonished him that he was allowed only one piece before bed, and he nodded in solemn agreement, knowing that he'd secreted a Mars bar from the Owens's house in his back pocket. The doorbell rang, and his parents looked at each other. Rod rose and grabbed the dwindling bowl of pastel-colored Smartees and loped toward the door. It was a warm night, so the trick-or-treaters were out in earnest. Some older kids, barely in costume, had been by now that the hour was getting late, but he knew better than to scold them. The Owens property down the street had been toilet-papered two years in a row, which likely explained why they were giving out such a generous amount of candy this year. His wife was dozing when he returned to the living room. The scene on the television screen was a gruesome one: monsters threatening a family trapped in their station wagon. Rod switched off the set. "Okay, gang, let's all go to bed."

Mikey begged his mother to let him keep his bag of candy in his room, promising not to eat any until tomorrow. Knowing that she would say no, he pretended to pout and stomped off to bed. He listened carefully as both his parents checked on him, and whispered their summaries of the day. He heard his mother shut their bedroom door as his father padded down the hall to the kitchen, likely to grab a beer before slipping into his den to do some last-minute drawing. When the house had settled, Mikey turned on the small television in his room and caught the final few minutes of the movie that was playing in the living room. He'd seen it last year and loved the scene that was now flickering before him: the wounded monsters flew off into the night sky, ready to return next Halloween. After some garish local commercials, the host of the late-night horror show, Mr. Moonlight, in ghoulish, pale makeup and a black cape that had seen better days, announced that the next feature would be *Bride of Frankenstein*. Rod turned down the sound so as not to alert his parents that he was still awake. He finished the Mars bar and, licking his fingers as the languid pulse of the film toyed with the shadows in his room, he reached beside his bed for the box of Pumpykins.

Rod flipped the record. He loved drawing to the Allman Brothers; the music made him feel like he was free, on the road, driving late at night. Their albums always put him in a relaxed, creative mood. He was surprised that he'd already finished his first beer by the time he'd settled in at his desk, and wondered when one or two beers had turned into a nightly six-pack. Regardless, the stories had flowed lately –he'd gone from submitting ideas to writing the entire scripts for the cartoons and illustrating the back of the boxes. Plus, his work on the commercials –it all meant more money. They now had two cars, and he and Carolyn had seriously discussed their next vacation being in Hawaii. Hawaii! He'd fretted so, having lost his lucky charm, that this continuation of fortuity made him confident in his talents. He drew Witchee and Hector Specter first. He always drew them first. There was something haunting about sketching Gourdy. He didn't know why, but he always drew him last.

Though he'd seen the movie before, *Bride of Frankenstein* gripped Mikey like a lurid dream; hypnotized by the black and white imagery, he absentmindedly gorged himself from the nearly empty box of Pumpykins. He'd saved this box just for Halloween night. Amazingly, it mainly contained mounds of the marshmallow pumpkins, with just a dusting of cereal. He popped the treats in his mouth as he fought off sleep. He didn't want his parents to come into his room in the morning and find the television still on -much less an empty box of cereal– they might make good on their oft-repeated threat to take the TV away.

He didn't want Halloween to end.

Rod drew in a fury of black ink. The music he heard was not coming from the stereo –the bizarre calliope of sounds that urged him on came in through an unseen window, one only open every so often, letting in timeless, midnight music from other places unnamed and forgotten by all but secret priests dutifully burning incense atop frozen mountains. He stopped, exhausted, sweaty, an array of crushed beer cans at his feet. Slack-jawed, he blinked at the monstrous images before him. Gourdy, the silly, befuddled leader of the Pumpykins, grew a menacing smile. Then he grew arms and legs. In the next blotched frame, he pushed aside a surprised Witchee and Hector Specter and stepped out of the Forest of Evil and onto a very familiar street. Rod blinked as he strained to follow the story only he could have drawn. Tears obscured his vision as he watched Gourdy saunter past a group of oblivious teens throwing reams of toilet paper into the trees on either side of the walkway leading to his neighbor's door. In the next frame, an innocent Mikey sat on his bed, munching away from a box of Pumpykins. Frankenstein approached his reluctant bride on the TV. Gourdy, his black frame now long like an expectant scarecrow, walked up to their house –*his* house– and rang the doorbell. Rod fell out of his chair and tried to call out "Carolyn," but could only muster something between a gasp and a dry swallow. Shame filled him as he momentarily looked down at the empty beer cans to see if one still might possess a swig or two to calm his rampaging nerves. He returned to the last page of the illustration, this hellish map: Mikey ambles up to the door and opens it. A giant, leering jack-o'-lantern looks down and tilts its grooved skull as if asking a question. Mikey nods eagerly but pauses, gesturing with his hand for the pumpkin-thing to wait. He races to the kitchen to retrieve the pillowcase filled with candy and slips out the door. Gourdy takes him by the hand, and they walk down the middle of the street, disappearing into the darkness.

"A local man, Rod Carver, was arrested for disorderly conduct October 31st, after several neighbors called to complain that he was harassing trick-or-treaters. Mr. Carver, divorced and unemployed, is no stranger to tragedy. His only child is believed to have been abducted twenty years ago, Halloween night. At the time police and the FBI combed the entire state and the case receives renewed attention every Halloween, in no small part due to Mr. Carver's annual activities. He is known to approach and attempt to unmask parents and children. His attorney stresses that Mr. Carver is receiving mental health counseling and renewed a request that anyone with information pertaining to the disappearance of Mikey Carver to please come forward."

—*Bizarre Assault Mars Festive Halloween*, Avondale Dealer, November 1st, 2002

Grey Salamanders

Among the Limehouse paperboys, Wilmot Reed (everyone called him Reed) stood out, and not just because he was tall. Before his mother passed, she had taught him basic manners and the supreme value of the pound. She had known far more than the common London whore, having received something of an education before her merchant father's financial ruin led him to suicide and her down into the oldest profession. Her bastard son had a bit more bearing about him than the usual urchin, as well as his unknown father's height. He picked up additional knowledge along the way, lessons learned in alleys, on rooftops, things not yet written in books. At least not yet.

The drunken sailors that wove the foggy Limehouse streets were easy targets for pickpockets, and if their trousers were filled with other morsels, Reed could help them there as well. Dank Limehouse public houses, close to the burgeoning docks of the Thames, attracted seamen from around the world. Gentlemen from the tonier parts of the city would occasionally partake as well, and not because the ale was cheap. Reed learned early that some men prefer the company of other men, and not just when they didn't have a purse for a whore or were so drunk they'd fuck anything that crossed their path. Others liked them *young*. As such, they assessed Reed's height to mean he was long in the cock as well, and they were always pleased to see the length he produced once the amount was settled. These extra shillings kept Reed alive and indoors many a damp winter. Now, he was nearly too old to attract that very specific lot and was about to age out as a paperboy as well.

He had spent the day hungry, looking for work on the docks without any luck, and settled at the most infamous night cellar in Limehouse, The Reversal, to drink away his last shillings. After he ordered a second glass of gin, a thin gentleman in an elegant dark tailcoat at the other end of the bar caught his eye.

That tavern was a black nexus of cracksmen, macers, toolers, palmers, and the mandrakes that favored such rough trade. Reed knew that the toffs, the more well-dressed, sometimes landed gentry even, prized discretion and communicated with a mere look, preferring low talk outside rather than barroom conversations overheard by blackmailers. Having met steady eyes with his own, a silent agreement was made. Both finished their drinks. He left after the gentleman, but not so quickly that anyone would make the connection. The night smelled of horse manure and the river. The river smelled of an ocean of toil, thick with the refuse of London sewers, all distilled into a lapping ribbon of desperation and sorrow. The gentleman turned and acknowledged his presence with a curt nod as he veered down an alley. Reed pursued, hopeful for more than a doorway fuck: being invited back to a fellow's rooms meant a proper wash and maybe a meal afterwards. As he turned the corner, the gentleman was waiting for him beside his waiting carriage, a highly polished black affair that, to the boy, screamed menace and money.

Why do the two always go together? He thought and wavered.

The man held his calling card up in the air. Reed instinctively reached for it, for any opportunity really, but the man held it higher aloft. The dim light of the streetlamp showed him to be only a few years older than Reed, though sallow cheeks and unfocused eyes implied vices the paperboy had yet to entertain.

"First things first. You're that lad who used to hawk papers, calling out the headlines near Euston Station?"

"Yes, sir!" He was thrilled that his mark knew him, might

have been nursing a long-held infatuation.

"Good, good, your timbre is excellent."

"My mother was an actress," he lied. "Long gone from the pox, I'm 'fraid." He added, instantly regretting the premature attempt to gain sympathy.

The man pointed a white, gloved finger at the soiled crotch of Reed's threadbare trousers.

"And no French gout? I don't like my sausage spoiled."

"No, sir, clean as a whistle!"

"Hmmmm, I bet you've had your whistle cleaned quite often. Well, never mind, I've steady work for a discreet boy. Present this card early in the morning at the address listed, and we'll see to it."

Reed stared at the whiteness of the card cradled in his soiled palm. He knew numbers, not letters, and decided to confess as much.

"To be expected, dear lad. Your education begins."

As the gentleman turned toward the waiting carriage, he whispered the street address. Reed's thoughts vacillated between his lack of lodgings for the night and the fact that the liquor he had consumed at The Reversal did little to quell his hunger. Also pressing was what, exactly, did his toff mean by *"education"*?

He felt both conspicuous and completely ignored on the streets of Arlington, one of the wealthiest, most exclusive neighborhoods in London. Reed was shocked that, after sleeping rough, in the small amount of time it took him to reach the intended address, he had not merely crossed streets but exchanged worlds. Rambling tenements had quickly given way to mansions, and sidewalks widened, paving stones righted themselves. The poor and desperate receded, and quiet and quick nobs dashed in every direction, even though dawn had barely broken.

Reed brushed away nonexistent dust from his filthy overcoat and again straightened the collar. The address he had been given was close to the park, on one of the more private lanes lined with fine coaches and militant doormen. As he approached and was about to produce the card, the door opened and a servant jerked his head – a silent signal that Reed should go around back. He did so, and the door opened as he mounted the steps, not as if the household awaited his arrival, but rather, such an appearance was routine.

A stoic butler awaited, his coat black and shiny like the midnight carriages rent boys enter, never to be seen again. The butler measured him with his eyes and stepped aside to usher him in. Reed was waved down an impossibly long and narrow hall and through a set of doors. The butler motioned for him to undress and wash himself in a steaming tub within the center of the room. He did so gladly, unsure of how long it had been since he had had a bath. As he exited, the gentleman from the previous night entered, still in his nightshirt, loose and womanly off his shoulder. He held a steeping cup of tea beneath his nostrils while circling the tub. Reed pretended at shyness, a hand before his elongated member but low, so ripe bush protruded above extended, chilblained knuckles. The gentleman gave a humored curtsy to this performance, so Reed let his hand drop and stood there, a wet anatomical specimen. His toff apparently appreciated candor and closed in for a closer look. The boy tried a steady, seductive gaze, but his observer was interested in something else.

"Right. You'll do just fine. Let's get you dressed and in the study. Pass through the kitchen on your way. I don't want to be distracted by stomach grumbles."

With that, he left the room, and the butler returned with a nightshirt and sack within which he gathered his filthy clothes.

Reed choked down a fistful of biscuits and strong tea at a table packed with other household servants who paid him no mind, offered not a word, and again he felt part of an unstated schedule. After Reed finished his meal, the butler reappeared and silently shepherded him down another long hallway with more turns than he felt a building should have a right to, and into a vast library. He gasped – so many books, with a brass ladder on wheels to reach the furthest ones. Books like stars, they were so far out of reach. His gentleman stood with pen in hand behind a music stand. The curtains were opened, and he looked pale in the sunlight, smaller without the cloak of night, sickly yet still regal.

"And now our labor. We may begin."

Reed gave a practiced leer and started to unbutton his nightshirt when the doors flew open and an elderly woman in a dark dress, her hair in a severe bun, entered.

"M'lord." She greeted the master of the house curtly and began fussing with a small tray of writing utensils and books.

"Boy, learn your lessons well, you're to do all that Nan asks, and she'll see you're fed, paid, and, if she reports back the appropriate progress, you'll be back for more, I dare say."

With that, he exaggeratedly bowed and exited the library. The governess turned and presented Reed with all the instruments with which a small child is taught to comprehend letters. The books on composition were shelved nearby. She began to march back and forth as she issued instructions, clarifying that she would not repeat herself, swatting the palm of her hand with a small brass whisk from the fireplace for punctuation. Insolence would be rewarded with a knock on his knuckles. He swallowed and stared at the large letters in the book. He recognized their shapes from the papers he had peddled, and concentrated on the amount of promised coin. His determined leer resurfaced; this was a much easier task than buggering that rotund Vicar whose thick buttocks made lancing his hole nigh impossible.

The sessions were no more taxing than working on the docks or suffering a large, dirty cock in his mouth, one attached to a macer too drunk to cum and too stupid to call it quits. His regular crew of rent boys at The Reversal were none the wiser, as he could not let on he was flush or every hand would be out. The best he could do was let the younger mates crash on the floor of his room with the promise that they pay him later, a debt he had no plans to collect if he could continue to put the squeeze on this lord. He longed to talk about it, however. Often, the boys would gather on a favorite rooftop and gossip over a jar of gin as dawn crept across London. They laughed about the odd things that toffs require to get off, though the way some of the lads pulled on their crotches during the round of stories diminished their derision. It was a survival instinct to know just how these scenes ended, and Reed was clueless. He was flummoxed on whether he should continue to improve on his own now that he could afford the penny dreadfuls that used to fascinate him, back when he could only stare at the illustrations through a shop window. If he improved too quickly, would the money run out? So far, that hadn't proven to be the case. As his letters had improved, the governess had moved on to elocution lessons. The lord was but a shadowy figure, present only in the mornings, a sleepy ghost floating over the proceedings, bleary-eyed but watchful that his investment was maturing at the right pace.

One morning, the lord lingered. Reed noticed that none of the writing instruments or school books were present. When the library door opened, instead of the governess, a young man entered the room. By his demeanor and dress, Reed guessed a stable boy.

"Good, good. You there, paperboy, you'll need to do just as I tell you, pose as for a painter, a painter of words."

With that, he took a long pull on his pipe, a queer, thin thing, and held his smoke, bookended between hollowed cheeks. As he exhaled, his eyes momentarily closed.

As the stableman unlaced his boots, the toff came to life and barked.

"You're in the stable, paperboy! Pretend you've snuck into the master's stable, to steal a nap."

Reed felt a heady mixture of excitement and relief: finally, things made sense. He had long ago mastered his body and was eager to show the lord what he could do. The lad opposite was a handsome sort and near his age. The smoke wafting through the room was sweeter than tobacco, darker, of midnight deserts and dreams best savored and then forgotten. He breathed deeply and imagined the emerald divan a bale of hay.

"Good, good! Now, lad, you're the master, mad that this ragamuffin is trespassing, and you know just the punishment he deserves. That's right, loosen your belt and storm the barn!"

He wrote furiously, damp hair matted to his brow, as the young men both took direction as well as improvised. Reed's shirt was above his head, the stable boy between his lifted legs, when a butler interrupted with tea service. The threesome took a break for cucumber sandwiches. The boys ate heartily while the toff kept spooning sugar into his tea until Reed thought that man would prefer a cup of white mud to teethe on. The stable boy looked content in his work, rearranging the plump stiffness in his trousers between bites of his sandwich. Reed was curious about what was being written and tried to peer around the corners of the music stand: the script was beautiful, black, like the lines of a map if maps traced song instead of streets. The story was different than the one being performed, however. Dark, manic deeds raced across the page. He furrowed his brow, trying to gather meaning from the erotic clouds racing up and down the sheets of paper; Reed was more interested in buggering the stable boy, however. The impoverished lad who shared his bed had rolled and stretched against his body all night, and Reed had yet to find release. He caught his eye and gave him a signal that the pantomime was over; the other boy looked relieved and stood and undressed. No matter the orders and directions the frustrated lord barked, they grappled with one another as it pleased them.

As his lessons decreased, Reed was asked back to the mansion by the park to stage a variety of scenes, often but not always with the same youth. One memorable performance concerned the suddenly shy stable boy and a young maid Reed had seen in the kitchen. In the library, she had been transformed into a Queen, using a bed sheet as a robe, a saucer as a crown, and ordering the boys to do certain things to her and each other with surprising relish. The meanings or settings of different scenarios were harder to pin down, but Reed took direction and looked to the obviously more experienced stable boy for guidance. There was no end to this sexual circus. He was well paid, and leaving the mansion one evening, he nicked a new coat from a neighbor's laundry line —so things were looking up. All of this, and the stable boy had a thick staff, and once Reed had figured out how to fit him inside, the boys couldn't keep their hands off each other.

The gentleman only ever stopped writing to pull on his own leaking lobcock or puff the pipe. Some afternoons, he would fall asleep on the divan. The naked Reed craved to run his fingers across the spines of the books, and maybe sample the sweetness of his lordship's pipe. Still, as if on cue, the dark butler always entered, silently directing them to dress, the stable boy back to work, Reed out of the house, palming a half schilling, far less than what the toff would have paid out had he remained awake and writing.

One morning, he was ushered into the library alone, no stable boy, no array of items meant to be arranged into a slave ship on the Nile, or, a favorite of late, a vicar accidentally locked in an insane asylum overnight. The shades were drawn, the air stale with sickly breath and old smoke. A shallow cough drew him toward the overturned music stand. His gentleman was sitting on the floor, head hung low.

"I'm too dissipated to do so myself."

Reed blinked, unsure.

The gentleman pointed limply toward the divan.

A bound manuscript was placed there, like a paper crown upon a velvet pillow.

"You must deliver it to the printer, Mr. Wright, posthaste. The address is there with the manuscript. I am too ill today. Go. He expects you and will pay you handsomely. Go."

Reed was quizzical but understood the importance and potential finality of the assignment. If the book his toff had been feverishly writing was done, then it was quite possible his visits to the mansion had drawn to an end. The printer was a source of future capital. With the weight of the manuscript in both hands, he slipped out of the room as once again, that prescient butler was there, holding the door.

He knew the street, he knew the business. Randy sailors would ask where they could buy "Socratic books," and it paid to be well-informed. He turned down an unnamed alley thick with foreign men sleeping in the doorways of opium dens. Upstairs from one such hovel was the print shop renowned for producing political tracts and poorly translated French pornography. He mounted the stairs two at a time and knocked lightly, forgetting that it was a business and not a private house.

"Come in!" A man roared from inside.

Reed sheepishly stepped into the shop. The air was thick with the smell of ink, cigar smoke, and perspiration. The printer was a compact, muscular man in a leather apron. His perfectly trimmed ink-black beard and mustache further shaped his already angular face. The thick lenses of his small, wire-framed glasses obscured his eyes.

"Place the manuscript on the floor."

He obeyed and stood there, awaiting further instructions, wondering how much he was to be paid.

"Disrobe. Place your clothes on that chair."

Now used to taking such instructions, Reed complied and, as he stepped out of his shabby underwear, just as he had so often in the presence of the stable boy, the memory of whom inspired his emerging erection to bob in the air. Pretending shyness, he bent forward and pulled his shoulders together as if he could fold into himself and conceal his sex. The printer did not appear to notice his act as he moved about the shop.

"Bend down. Down on all fours."

Reed obeyed. The dirty floor was cold, filmy with inky dust.

"Put your arse up, put your nose in the book."

Reed pivoted on his knees and put his face close to the bound package of writing. The head of his cock thudded against the floor, leaving a musty ectoplasmic fingerprint of pre-cum in the dust. He felt exposed, like a hungry dog on a narrowing street.

"Untie it and read aloud while I close up shop."

Reed balanced himself on one elbow as he struggled to untie the manuscript and maintain his position on all fours. Cool air caressed his bare ass; his penis lengthened further and again grazed the floor. He shuddered as the words on the page came into focus. The slender, grey salamanders of opium smoke shimmied up through the floorboards. Such words. Delicate script, the wake of a silent ship calmly fording a deep, unexplored ocean of lust. A boot pushed his knees farther apart. He jumped as cool leather met warm flesh.

"I want to hear your voice, I want to see the words."

The first paragraph described incestuous acts between brothers. An erotic shiver launched up his spine as he recalled achieving these very positions with the stable boy. He heard the door lock, and the "open" sign turned around. Shades were pulled. The man paced.

"Read on."

The next passage described a youth tenderly washing the elongated penis of a massive, stationary stallion. The printer loomed behind him as he continued to read haltingly. He felt a sensation between his legs and arched his back. A momentary finger, rounded, smooth: gloved? -pressed against his clenched ass and retreated. His cock quivered.

"Use your mouth to turn the page."

The boy tilted his head and pondered. A boot applied slight pressure to the spread of his fingers on the floor, so he quickly licked his lips and turned a page with his tongue. Several pages clung together and fell as a whole; he braced himself for unknown punishment. Either the printer didn't notice or didn't care. He again read aloud.

This new passage concerned a naked boy on all fours on the floor of a bookshop, reading aloud.

Reed shuddered as Mr. Wright circled him. Silver wisps of opium curled up from the shadowy den below. As he read, the printer withdrew a quill from its stand, moistened it on his tongue, and inserted it in his supplicant's rear.

As Reed read those very words aloud, gloved fingers pressed the writing utensil further in. He stammered but knew that where there was a glove, there was a boot, so with a whisper, he continued the story of the boy's ecstasy, and as described on the page, a pinion wound its way inside him.

"He expects you and will pay you handsomely." Yet his gentleman said he had planned on going himself, but fell ill.

Like every Limehouse paperboy, he'd buggered and been buggered. Before the stable boy's ample staff, there were back-alley assignations for a sixpence, flophouse floors for warmth. This was different. As he read and as the quill traveled farther in, he felt its original feather form return and multiply into the lush wing of a golden griffin. He wanted to lie completely still and focus on this new and painful pleasure, but the hand now on his neck steered him to read, and the words poured out, and his cock ached, and an effusive, molten heat dribbled forth, quickly caught by an extended finger and fed back to him.

His tongue, no longer dry, turned the page.

Here was a sonnet about a sonnet written in blood, and Reed did not follow the meaning of the poem, though his whole body shivered as the printer's circling pace around him quickened.

The quill was still inside him, and he arched his back further, as if he could ignite the griffin's pinion into full wings when, really, the hand of a practiced falconer was required.

That gloved hand returned, hovering near his testicles. He tensed. Once, an overweight gentleman in a top hat had offered him ten shillings to get in the back of his hansom cab, and Reed eagerly complied, loosening his trousers as the driver shut the door. The older man, inebriated, his beard woolly with spilt snuff, pulled Reed's pants down and clutched his sac with such brutality that the youth cried and kicked his way out of the lurching cab, naked from the waist down, which set the whores of Charing Cross laughing.

The grip on his neck tightened. Face against the page, he could see the imperfections of the ink as lines began to stretch and yearn, like branches reaching for the sun. The letters pulsed and opened as if hungry flowers. Still, he read. A stack of books in the corner shimmered as if about to disassemble, paper into sand, the printed words angry mad ants that would ravage the room.

Reading aloud a passage wherein a mad Queen tortured two servant boys, he tripped over the word "cunt" and, with a guttural laugh, the printer entered him roughly, pushing forward, heavy and brutish in his rhythm. Cheek on the floor, pages scattered, and still he read aloud. Fading purple smoke from below filled his nostrils. One leg bent, the other outstretched, he clutched the nearest sheet of paper and read, words punctuated by the grunting man riding him hard. Eyes tearing, the letters went in and out of focus as his penis thickened. Pages fluttered across the room, out of reach, the printer grunting above. So he read the titles off the spines of the books on the shelves. He gasped and gulped, and in between his recitations, he listened for the flap of griffin wings.

Mr. Wright lifted him roughly off the floor and turned him over and straddled his naked body, now coated in sweat. He held Reed's head by his damp hair with one hand while he pulled on his own cock with the other. The boy parted his lips just as the printer unfurled in his mouth, and Reed's semen shot out and onto the floor, hitting loose pages of manuscript. The printer's glasses fell, and anger crossed his face. His eyes were, in turn, wild and distant. He was blind. He collapsed on top of Reed. His weight crushed the boy's face into the separated pages of the manuscript.

A key worked the door as Reed struggled beneath the bodily press of the printer.

The butler entered and locked the door. Reed panicked and fought to stand up. The butler set a doctor's case down and pulled out a white rag and a clear bottle.

He approached and knelt before the fraught boy.

"Calm down, son, calm down. This won't hurt at all. Apparently, the eyes don't have nerves, as luck would have it."

He dabbed some of the liquid onto the cloth.

"Can't blackmail someone if you can't see the materials 'tis all. You're about to learn a new trade."

Shoe on a scrap of the manuscript, he leaned in. The boy's cheek was slick with his own white splatter, an inverse to the black looping cursive script that told his story. The last one he would ever read.

Night Market

Having relocated for work to Japan, Matthew did not expect to find the single most important, valuable, and rarest of anime treasures in a crate of discarded VHS tapes in one of the seedier night markets of Bangkok. He had thumbed through the tattered collection only to kill time as his traveling companion pretended to haggle over a piece of electronic equipment that he had every intention of buying, regardless the price, the exchange rate being so in his favor. Really, the haggling was just to get into the swing of things, much to the consternation of the skinny youth who ran the stall and assumed all foreigners were wealthy, and was therefore flummoxed by the unnecessary dispute over price. Second-rate Japanese porn never held Matthew's interest. As much as he was attracted to Japanese men, the pixilated private parts ruined any eroticism and rendered him numb, no matter the gymnastics taking place on film. Still, porn is porn. He flipped through the selection, and actually bypassed the video in question, its existence so rumored, its capture so impossible to imagine, this genuine white whale of erotic anime, that he thought the spermy explosions on the cover, the university student's pummeled buttocks spread open by lustful, leering jocks, the surge of menacing appendages, just another heterosexual fantasy of a particularly Japanese variety. Recognition kicked in, and he blinked and froze. His thoughts raced back to online message boards, rumors of a deeper realm of X-rated gay anime than he and his fellow obsessives had yet been able to download and trade. Only one blurry, oft-reproduced image from a mail-order catalog in the 90s served as proof that the film actually existed: the same picture he had just seen, but now in full, vivid color. The box was much handled, but, as he carefully shook the tape loose and examined it, he found a near-perfect original copy. He clutched the VHS cassette in both hands as he approached the young man who feigned defeat over the agreed-upon price his friend had just countered. As money was exchanged, he counted out the appropriate Bhat - not wanting to discuss price or in any way create an opening where the tape in question wasn't immediately, irrevocably his. The young man flashed a relieved grin, separating the wispy strands of his mustache even further, and gladly completed the haggle-free purchase with a bow, repeating in a sing-song voice likely perfected for Caucasian tourists. "You like, you like, very good, very good!" Matthew wondered if he would have said that about any of the tapes available, or if he had an inkling of the unique darkness that unwound on the cassette now wrapped tightly in a recycled plastic fast-food bag.

Both travelers leaned back, content in their seats as the plane took off. Matthew wiped lingering sweat from his brow and ordered a ginger ale to help diminish his hangover. Aki, his acquaintance from the bar, who had surprisingly invited him on this trip, had already fallen asleep and even snored lightly, his battered Supreme baseball cap pulled down over his eyes. They were drinking buddies at the only gay bar in Matthew's neighborhood, a boring suburb of Yokohama, where his company housed employees. At first, he was disappointed not to be in the heart of Tokyo, but he had quickly grown to value the area's small charms, and alternately ate dinner in the same three restaurants, though when he came home drunk after required happy hour outings with co-workers, he was satiated by the take-out at the Seven-Eleven across the street from his tidy apartment complex. He was happily surprised to find the chain not only everywhere in Japan, but that it possessed first-rate food. He liked that they sold shirts and ties in plastic bags for the salary men who passed out drunk in parks and needed a fresh set of clothes for work the next day. The only disappointment was the manga was limited to teenage boy stuff: stories about sports heroes and eating competitions, as far as he could tell. Thankfully, the more hardcore stuff was available at local bookstores everywhere, and he was shocked that he had to share the aisle with young women. School girls casually read gay pornography on the train. While stateside, he had obsessed over specific subgenres and was able to find much of what appealed to him, not only for free but translated, so he expected his arrival in Japan to be something like sliding into the pink whorl of a throbbing cornucopia: unimagined sexual treats always at hand. Instead, he was frustrated that the manga here was shrink-wrapped, so he could never tell what he was getting until he got home, and then it was in Japanese, of course, which didn't exactly stymie him, but it didn't add to the allure and often left him confused.

Aki's invitation to travel to Bangkok for a weekend had come as a surprise, and traveling with such a casual acquaintance wasn't typical for him. Still, Matthew knew from the gay guides that Japanese gay men tend to make their friends in such bars, and as a matter of etiquette, the invitation was sincere. After all, Matthew craved adventure, and Bangkok was a place where excitement could be found or purchased. It turned out that Aki had been many times, knew fantastic food stalls where they gorged on pad thai for the price of roughly one dollar each, and spent hours every night in an infamous bathhouse where you picked your preferred prostitute out of a line-up by the number on a tag affixed to the scanty white towel wrapped around their golden waists. Every time Matthew passed Aki in the hall or bumped into him in the steam room, Aki would give him an expressive thumbs up and describe his latest sexual conquest in perfect, business-like English. The trip was already memorable; the afterthought of their shopping at the touristy night market had resulted in the discovery of a lifetime, and they were so excited that, unlike Aki, Matthew couldn't take a much-needed nap. As the stewardess jostled down the aisle behind a clinking cart of miniature bottles, Matthew suppressed the urge to squeeze past Aki and check on the cassette in the overhead bin, to caress it and reconfirm his good fortune. As sleep evaded him, his thoughts turned to more practical matters, like how to procure a VCR.

At work, Matthew correlated the latest figures from the India team and dumped his analysis into the monthly report. He had already plotted his course to Akihabara, the otaku neighborhood, and had discussed with colleagues at lunch which mammoth retailer was likely to still sell working VCRs. One of the more interesting aspects of the Japanese is that they are, as a whole, inveterate collectors. Tower Records, long gone the way of the big box store dinosaurs of the last century in the US, were still omnipresent in urban Japan, stocked with music from the U.K. and the U.S. There were record stores everywhere, and even specialty shops where you could rent used CDs to copy at home. He was the first one out of the office that night. It was still light out as he threaded the throngs of weary commuters.

From the first scene, the video convulsed with purple tentacles lashing supple buttocks. Any time a male mouth opened in cries of protestation or rapture, the fleshy tip of a tentacle filled the orifice, the pucker of every sucker a violent pair of lips. Matthew was in his underwear and undershirt when the video started and was quickly naked as the film progressed. The fable behind the onslaught began to come into focus: an ancient race of beings had been awoken when the Tori that had blocked their entry into the surface world had been unceremoniously removed to make way for a new high school gymnasium. That night, they infiltrated the plumbing and shot out of the drains to possess the boys' soccer team en masse —boys who now roamed the halls ready to unleash their possessed penises on the unsuspecting school body. Drunk, engorged, Matthew spread his sweaty legs wide on the tatami mat. He stroked himself slowly, not wanting the ecstasy of this discovery to come to fruition, knowing that if it did, though, he would be able to tease out a second watery orgasm, and then punish his rendered meat for a third time if need be.

What quality! This was superior filmmaking and not cheap, thoughtless pornography. The movie possessed all the stylized animation of Satoshi Kon's feature films, their lush attention to detail, the artful and fluid ways scenes progress, more like a painting than a cartoon. The richness of the colors was particularly startling. Especially the color red. It began *in media res*: no title, no opening credits. So few people had seen the film that the commentary online offered scant information on who actually made this masterpiece. On the screen, one of the jocks' eyes rolled back in his head as a tentacle tongue swept out of his mouth and wrote in Japanese on the fogged bathroom mirror.

Matthew hoisted an elongated pearl of pre-cum to his dry lips and stared at the un-translated kanji symbol. He intuited that it meant "more."

The speckled nerd who stumbled out of the library and into the arms of the naked and waiting jock horde was flailed by tentacles, which dexterously removed his school uniform and re-affixed his glasses so he could witness the brutal assault that was about to be visited upon his virgin hole.

Matthew placed the cool lips of the empty beer bottle against the knuckle of his sphincter and released his hard cock, lest he cum right then and there.

The scene on the tape switched to a mountaintop temple. A young monk sat before the giant wooden statue of a penis suspended from the ceiling. His eyes closed in meditation. Resolute, he rises, grabs his staff, and tightens his robe. As he leaves, behind him, the huge phallus rocks back and forth.

He runs one finger up and down the stiff underbelly of his cock, and pushes the bottle away. He puts his thumb in his mouth and imagines that fat cock he sucked in the steam room at the Bangkok bathhouse, the abundant foreskin swishing around in his mouth like new silk sheets in a washing machine. The money boy's legs wrapped around his body, the prostitute signaling to him that he was on break, that this was his way of relaxing between tricks, Matthew more than willing to oblige, lips pressed against tight belly and fleshy thighs, and the whole of the rigid cock pulsed within the grip of his tongue.

The rotating tentacle that filled the geek's cavity lifted his naked body in unison with the thick protuberance that stretched his mouth. Shoes dropped, slender feet and arms hopelessly flail. The jocks that wielded these impressive appendages steadied themselves, legs apart and arms out, drooling vehicles of possession as sperm shot out of the boy's nearly hairless, tiny cock. The doors to the library fly open as the monk floats in, and light shoots out of his golden, glowing wooden staff.

Orgasm mounting, Matthew thought wildly about the other men in the steam room who encircled him as the prostitute rose and patted him on the top of his head. Towels dropped, forming a damp nest around him as cocks of varying size and circumference were presented. He took the closest in his mouth to the root, gripping the others in his hands, pulling the growing crowd closer to him by moving from cock to cock with his tongue, sensing who would be satisfied with a quick lick, who needed to be taken in fully and expertly nursed to better root them to their spot, the better to wed this circle to him, to gain time to assess their individual needs and orchestrate their collective orgasms. He left the bathhouse hours later, with a giddy Aki at his side. When Aki pressed him on how many men he had, he pretended not to understand, as, having lost count, he had surpassed the number that most equates with pure ecstasy.

A massive, demonic, green god rode the clouds in the night sky above the school, and the monk froze in the fiery beams of his stare. The story became confusing as all linear elements dissipated and scene after scene of sexual abandon filled the screen: a man walking down the street with a lascivious crimson tentacle curling and uncurling from the open fly of his navy blue business suit. The jocks playing basketball, dribbling and shooting hoops with their tentacle arms while their roiling, throbbing cock-tentacles take turns fucking every pleading orifice of their diminutive coach, naked and tied to the post. A newscaster, shaking, tries to calm the populace as news of the tentacle outbreak terrifies the city, but before he can get another word out, tentacles erupt out of his mouth and rush the camera.

Back arched, Matthew licks his thumb, sticks it in his ass, and marvels at the high arc his cum makes before splattering his ankles and the floor. He's heaving, his chest wet with sweat. He wants to shower, to stop the treasured tape, but he's too entranced and falls back. Mindlessly fingering the drops of cum that dot his thigh, he watches on.

Aggrieved parents gather and barricade themselves in the temple. One mother passes out dumplings. As the shocked and bewildered congregation unwrap their food, her arms turn into hypnotically writhing tentacles. She goes over to caress the giant phallus, whispering into its carved pucker. It glows purple and starts to lengthen.

Matthew stumbles over to the small refrigerator and is

disappointed that there's no more beer. He remembers some cheap Seven-Eleven whiskey he stashed in the cupboard with the single bowl and plate that came with the apartment. He drinks from the bottle, and it burns the back of his throat. The images on the screen blur, and he can't decide if he should go online and see if he can find someone to come over and fuck his mouth, or keep watching the unfolding sexual kaleidoscope before him. He rewinds the tape bit, paranoid such an act might damage it, back to before he went to the kitchen, but can't seem to find that part of the story; it whirls backwards in grainy waves of snowy fallout, but every time he stops the tape, it's an unfamiliar vignette:

The statue of the phallus begins to swing back and forth, and in doing so, twin tentacles sprout from beneath the scrotum, so when it breaks free, it's able to support itself.

Fast forward.

The coach blows his whistle, and the jocks, healthy human bodies in tight red shorts, each with a thick tentacle unfurling from where their neck and head should be, run through a field of tires as bored cheerleaders chew gum and check their glowing phones.

Rewind.

A live-action scene: A young man in baggy sweatpants and shiny new unlaced sneakers sends a text message: 'I'm outside.'

The instant reply: door open.

He lets himself into a dark apartment. It's Matthew's apartment.

Kicking off his shoes, he uses his phone to light the way to the bedroom. The mattress on the floor quivers a bit as he strips. Naked, he pulls back the sheets, and a mass of tentacles explodes, seizing him.

Rewind.

Live-action: he and Aki at the night market, hunched over a bowl of steaming noodles. Aki laughs - a strand of noodle dangles from his chopsticks. The noodle wiggles a bit and then expands at its base into a small, menacing tentacle. Matthew looks down at his bowl -the fleshy mass of tentacles before him struggles to unknot itself.

He quickly shuts the TV off, turns off the VCR, unplugs both for good measure, and breathes deeply. He knows he's drunk and likely dehydrated, but goes back to the kitchen and takes the whiskey out of the cabinet. The ice tray in the freezer is one of those antiquated metallic kind where you have to pull a lever to emancipate the cubes, oddly archaic for a country that seems on the verge of inventing teleportation. Having an opinion about something other than what he just witnessed goes a long way toward calming his nerves. He pours himself a drink and goes to the bathroom to start the shower. Matthew needs the water on his back and neck to further return to reality. In the shower, he thinks about stepping out for a while, going down the street to Yoshinoya for a quick bowl of rice and thin slices of beef. Maybe text Aki and see if he's still up.

As Matthew strenuously scrubs away any remaining semen still glued to his ankle, in the other room, the VCR cord quivers to life. As does the cord to the television. Both roil and stretch, rubbing against each other in a serpentine way before nosing across the floor and plugging themselves back in. The television blinks to life as the tape dutifully begins to rewind. With the door closed and the rush of water, Matthew doesn't hear this whir and click as the film unspools loops of glistening black tape out of the mechanical crevice of the VCR. He shuts the water off and reaches for the MUJI towel as the slick accumulation plops onto the floor and undulates as if it were deep beneath the ocean, making its way across a calm and sandy seabed. Matthew towels his hair and tentatively thinks about how he can copy the tape to DVD and sell copies online for a tidy profit when the bathroom door opens. He spins in horror as something hard and slimy grips his ankles, fills his mouth, covers his eyes, and pries at his anus. Heart beating as fast as it ever has -his flagging cock twitches back to life. Tumescent, constricted, blind, he knows this is his time to surrender, to bend just so, the jackknife of his body lets everything in, just as he has done in the past with lovers at college and in various apartments and with strangers in late-night parking lot toilets.

At work, Matthew correlated the latest figures from the India team and dumped his analysis into the monthly report. He looks a bit wan but otherwise none the worse for wear. Today he'll join his colleagues in the cafeteria. He'd packed his own lunch this time, though he'll grab a soda from one of the ubiquitous vending machines in the hallway. Not that he's hungry. At least not in the usual sense. Matthew can feel the contents of the plastic container pulsing impatiently in his briefcase, ready to burst forth and unwind, multiply, burrow, and expand, consuming everything in its path.

You Decide How Much Is Enough

Halifax Supplemental Incorporated Internal Memo
Somyr™ Initial Marketing Meeting Minutes 1.12.39

Somyr tests exceptionally well and can be marketed as the only "timed" sleep aid available on the market. By that, we mean that doses can be measured, allowing the customer to decide on a sleep duration of anywhere from one to eight hours, based on the amount ingested per body weight.

Concerns: image of body on package to connote weight x dose should not be stigmatizing to the overweight.

Concept: pills shaped as moons and stars (argument against this is that the FDA will rule these easily mistaken for candy by children.)

Initial Advertising design: Smiling wrist watch with moons and stars instead of numbers. Slogan: "You Decide How Much Is Enough."

Advertising budget and rollout timeline in e-dropbin.

Note: future meetings with finance and development should not be scheduled back-to-back.

Additional note: online advertisements should target college students.

Somyr Trial Notes: Final
Entered into Hali-facts™ database 1.30.39

Final Test Trial: 12 subjects with a control group of equal number.

All subjects reported little to no drowsiness upon waking. Elevated serotonin levels in four subjects equate to normal bodily response to restive sleep. Additional trials strongly urged as two of the three male non-control group participants commented on unusual erotic thoughts.

Somyr Trials Notes: Additional
Entered into Hali-facts™ database 2.24.39

Additional Test Trial: 24 subjects with a control group of equal number.

All subjects in both groups are male. Subjects given a spectrum of Somyr doses. Four subjects across the dose spectrum reported unusual (to them) homosexual "feelings and thoughts" after waking. No reports of sexual dreams or discharge; reporting subjects expressed surprise but no negative impressions. It was deemed inappropriate to ask participants if they were heterosexual. Project Manager recommends production schedule suspended, Compliance Department notified.

Senior Vice President of Production Email 2.24.39

Production schedule suspension request denied.
Do not notify Compliance.
Additional testing approved/no overtime allowed.
Privileged/Confidential information may be contained in this message and may be subject to legal privilege. Access to this e-mail by anyone other than the intended recipient is unauthorized. If you are not the intended recipient (or responsible for delivery of the message to such person), you may not use, copy, distribute, or deliver to anyone this message (or any part of its contents) or take any action in reliance on

it. In such case, you should destroy this message, and notify us immediately. If you have received this email in error, please notify Halifax Supplemental immediately, and delete the e-mail from any computer. The views, opinions, conclusions, and other information expressed in this electronic mail are not given or endorsed by Halifax Supplemental unless otherwise indicated by an authorized representative independent of this message.

Research and Development Q2 Report 4.1.39 Somyr Excerpt

A previously unidentified side effect, "incidental homosexuality," has been reported by a minority of male test subjects. These "feelings" were fleeting, inconsequential, and should not impact the extremely positive viability of this product: the first over-the-counter sleep aid that the customer controls, with no other adverse side effects.

District Sales Manager email 7.1.39
Re:re:re:re: Las Vegas Sales Conference Agenda

Jake, GREAT buffet, had never been to the Wynn before, thought that side of the strip was dead. Certainly proved otherwise! Thanks, and thanks for presenting on teamwork. Your comment that commission is earned, not expected, should be burned into plaques and hung above every doorway at HQ.

New product rollouts all good. Almost. Somyr. Do ppl in R&D watch TV? The late-night comedians will rip this one to shreds. I'm not going to ask my reps to push this, it's just too weird.

Next conference call let's both be silent on last Q's #'s- our efforts speak for themselves so let the Pacific side talk their way out of this one!

Cheers,
Mike
PS. I like your new intern A LOT. Is she old enough to fly

without a parent? LOL

Dear Mike,

Again, all of your questions will be answered in the severance package mailed to your address on file. It's important to reiterate that this decision is final and non-debatable, so we are asking you to stop calling the office and to take a moment to reflect on the next chapter of your career. Your final check is included with the package, and we have copied and highlighted the relevant portions of the nondisclosure agreement you signed upon accepting employment with us.

We will not be responding to further emails from you.

Halifax thanks you for your service.
Halifax Supplemental Inc. Human Resources Department

Research and Development Meeting Notes 10.1.39

Conclusion to be communicated out to relevant departments: the Somyr side-effect is of the behavioral class and in no way as stigmatizing as the bevy of issues many anti-retrovirals present. It's worth noting that the initial version of the first male birth control pill had a low risk of "gambling tendencies" that did attract negative attention in the media while outperforming first-quarter expectations by 100%.

Alternative approach: market only to women and reduce fiscal year projections by approximately 50%.

Two interesting case studies on the male birth control pill and media fallout attached.

Marketing Department email 10.1.39
Re:re:re: Research and Development Meeting Notes

Another thought, if marketing only to women, why not a lavender-scented cotton stopper? I've read a lot of research lately on how certain scents influence purchasing decisions. Will forward article.

Also, Somyr sounds like the name of a car. If focusing on women would recommend something more feminine yet empowering.

Marta

Senior Vice President of Production Email 10.1.39

R&D: Somyr: proceed as planned.

Marketing: I like out-of-the-box thinking, but with this one, we need to be a bit more neutral. FDA hates bells and whistles. No TV commercials, print ads only.

Conclude testing phase.

New Senior Vice President of Production All Staff Email 10.3.39

I want to thank everyone for their patience and professionalism during this period of transition. I want to particularly thank my predecessor: everyone I've met so far is a dedicated team player and that says a lot about the shoes I have to fill.

I'll be coming by everyone's department in the coming weeks to introduce myself and learn more about your current projects, etc.

Looking forward to really getting to know the Halifax Supplemental Family.

Distribution folk: for now let's place Somyr in secondary markets only.

Marketing: please suspend anything English-language in the works. Contract out as needed per region. See new budgetary guidelines attached.

Open to new strategies on tomorrow's deep dive sales call, so please bring vibrant ideas :)

State Department Central sub-Saharan Africa Briefing Excerpt/ Classified 11.24.39

The so-called "Miracle of the Congo" continues at an unabated pace. The government, in an abrupt about face, has continued to promote a strongly liberal social agenda while only moderately repressing conservative religious leaders on the local level, often via well-placed exposés concerning sexual misconduct and/or bribery/a misuse of funds. A Bill of Individual Rights has been introduced in the newly reinvigorated Congress, and all political prisoners have not only been released and pardoned, but an international scholarship fund has been created for their children. International business relations have all been conscientiously improved, while the majority of police action has pivoted from social concerns to cases concerning graft among government officials. New libraries have been opened/proposed at an unprecedented pace, often involving top world-class architects as well as local talent; a progressive tax system has been introduced and laws negatively impacting

78

the press and social liberties canceled outright.

Openness to Western ideology in the Congo is something the US government should invest in heavily and soon, as the Chinese will likely seek countermeasures. The Chinese are heavily invested in the area and already believe covert American involvement is the root cause for these current changes.

The European ambassadorial class confirms rumors that President Rwenzori survived a suicide attempt sometime shortly after New Year's Eve, an apparent overdose on an unspecified sleep aid. If a brush with death ignited this change, then so be it. The positives have been vast and sweeping, and US engagement/support at the highest level is called for. Some actions are indeed harder to explain -his directive to paint all of the 747s in the Congolese National Airline fleet mauve, for instance. But the Democratic Republic of Congo, after decades of chaos and policy failures, now has a GDP rate of 25% per quarter, so whatever the cause, we would do well to bottle and distribute it.

Good Gelding

Decimus Lannerus despised the emperor, more so than the many, many other Romans who hated Tiberius. After all, the Emperor Tiberius was his employer. And unlike the vast network of military personnel, government functionaries, imperial palace officials, and assorted slaves and lackeys, Lannerus had direct, regular contact. Hating a tyrant from afar is a somewhat academic affair: table talk, bitterly delivered opinions meant to demonstrate your regard for the faded glories of the now thoroughly extinct Republic. It's different when he pays you (somewhat miserly, it should be noted) directly for your services. Worse, Lannerus was regularly in the presence of his despicable lapdogs, in particular the current Praetorian Prefect, the lethargic, seemingly slow-witted, paradoxically named Mercurius. A more reptilian man had yet to haunt the halls of the Senate (where he was reviled nearly as much as his predecessor, the publicly executed Sejanus). As it has been years since the Emperor had set foot in Rome, Mercurius frequently traveled back and forth between the island of Capri and the capital, delivering terror and intrigue, often with enough political dexterity that Lannerus, among others, held the opinion that he only feigned ignorance and ineptitude to better survive the imperial suspicion that had led to the wholesale slaughter of enemies perceived and imagined, including victims within Tiberius' own bloodline. While in Capri, he oversaw much of the daily operations of the Villa Jovis. While the Emperor had twelve such lavish estates majestically sprinkled across the island, this pleasure palace, owing mostly to the dark allure of the Grotta Azzurra, the subterranean playground was where the increasingly reclusive and debauched Tiberius resided.

When the much-revered Emperor Augustus was still alive and Tiberius was then his stepson (and later adopted son), he was a young general of some promise, much endeared to the troops who had given him the nickname "Biberius" due to the copious amount of wine he drank. The moniker was much in use now on Capri, though in whispered reference to a different substance, one he greedily sucked from the stamen of adolescent slave boys, more often than not dressed as Ganymede. Mercurius kept the island boys in wine and coin, ushering them in and out of the grotto every night. Those with stamina, or the good fortune to produce prodigious amounts of seed, were kept overnight and might, over time, with generous compensation to their parents, be inducted into his stable of prostitutes, circus performers, acrobats, weird twins, exotic and well-endowed slaves from the farthest corners of the empire, as well as a prized coterie of fey albinos, white creatures allergic to the very sun who made the grotto their home and never again saw the light of day. "My minnows," as this erotic menagerie was so named by the emperor himself.

Another point of interest that made the Villa Jovis the preferred imperial abode: it was the highest point on the Isle of Capri, looming over the rocky shore below and the dark ocean beyond as surely as the emperor loomed over Rome and empire. Several former Praetorian Prefects, luckless messengers bearing bad news and wealthy senators with estates worth confiscating had met their fate, midnight or after, on those very rocks. Lannerus prayed nightly to the Gods that Mercurius might likewise soon take flight.

While Lannerus oversaw the stable of horses that served all of the imperial properties, which was thankfully situated far from the cliffs that housed the Villa Jovis and close to the vast fields of grass at the island's center, the better to exercise the steeds, he was known to Tiberius from early in his career. Doomed by a stoic nature and a good reputation among the Praetorians, Lannerus rose through the ranks and gained the attention of the emperor, who took a deep pleasure in undermining such men. Much like a determined seagull will work over a tough, barnacled oyster every which way until finally prying it open, so too did Tiberius peck at every man under his command with the singular goal of dislodging his very sense of self. With his beliefs and reputation battered, until finally his soul was as exposed and fragile as the oyster's delicate inner gelatinous gray muck -only then would Tiberius be satisfied. A particular thin smile would cross his face, waver, and recede as he again scanned the room for his next prestigious victim.

Lannerus had a small army of slaves to feed and exercise the horses, and in his employ were stable hands and blacksmiths from the minute village nearby, eager for the work. The wealthy elite who had once populated the island during the fair winter months had slowly withdrawn as the emperor descended into debauchery, lest their sons and daughters be exposed to his wanton lust. The island was populated by empty villas and unemployed men given over to cheap drink and slanderous gossip.

Tiberius ensured that the islanders overheard his conversations with Lannerus, and peppered their talk with overly familiar terminology hinting at a deeper involvement on Lannerus' part in imperial proclivities. After these exchanges, if Lannerus were to proclaim his innocence to his subordinates, he would only look that much more guilty. So, he quietly fumed as Tiberius guffawed and winked and even, once, slapped his back in false merriment. It was like being struck by a dead mullet. He couldn't help but shudder, and to his surprise, Tiberius's sallow face lit with glee: after all, what makes for more delicious joy for the spider than seeing that the fly knows he's caught?

Now a septuagenarian, the emperor had given up the horseback riding he was so enamored with throughout his military career, but he still possessed an interest and fascination with animal husbandry that not only vexed Lannerus but made him of further value; when Mercurius himself summoned him to the Villa Jovis, Lannerus knew what grim task lay ahead and brought the necessary tools. Other times, if the messenger was a slave, he intuited that he was being brought to bear witness to the orgiastic proceedings within the dank confines of the Grotta Azzurra. Tiberius took additional pleasure in being observed by men of stature and pedigree who found his escapades especially revolting. The grotto contained multiple pools for frolic and depravity, and a collection of priapic statuary, some from ancient Athens, others from lands newly conquered. The emperor was known to have newly acquired slaves mount some of the more engorged members as a way of initiation. The pools were naturally replenished by the tides; the caverns were dark, except for the intermittent torchlight. Occasionally, the orgies were accompanied by blindfolded musicians. The blindfolds were less to keep the players from observing the wicked affair and more to heighten their fears as they could only imagine the sources of such aggrieved panting, the rare gleeful burst, and the smattering of painful cries. This added a wanton urgency to the underground music, which pleased the emperor to no end.

At dusk, Lannerus was observing the frolicking foals and assessing their future potential when he saw the familiar shape of Mercurius crossing the green field. A ship had just entered the shallow harbor that morning, carrying messengers from Rome, as well as merchants with goods to sell to the remaining villagers and farmers. Deep within the hull, a fresh crop of slaves remained until nightfall before disembarking at the Villa Jovis. The major domus preferred this mode of departure so that household slaves would only ever know the interior of the palace, thus less chance of a successful escape.

Before Mercurius was within earshot, Lannerus retrieved his tools and met him mid-field as the sun continued to set.

They were crowded into a cramped, low-ceilinged expanse, one of the grotto's larger antechambers amid a variety of secret rooms. Mercurius poured Lannerus a cup of wine and proceeded to take a deep drink himself, as if he were somehow steeling himself for the tasks ahead, as if his tastes were any less depraved than the emperor he served. The slaves were brought into the chamber and separated into two distinct groups: those who would work in the household, primarily the kitchen, and those who would join the aquatic basement brothel. Lannerus repressed a shiver at how young some of the future denizens appeared to be, though he knew that among them there were artisans of their "craft" and affected youthful demeanors and appearances, epilating pubic hair and whatnot, to better attract clients. He was surprised at how swiftly Mercurius moved to yank the youngest male out of line and place him among the household staff, whispering sharply "scullery boy" to the major domo. Not a moment too soon, as a hush descended and Tiberius and his ever-changing retinue of messengers, astrologers, and various slaves swooped into the room, not unlike a dark flock of vultures, an observation Lannerus had made on multiple occasions. This many people, and the torchlight dimmed and flickered. The emperor ignored the line of quaking household slaves and examined the recruits as if they were young soldiers about to enter battle. He pinched ass and measured cock, pulled on tongues, and harshly squeezed the breasts of the girls in the queue. Fear kept everyone in line. Inspection over, Tiberius gestured with an unusual flourish, and servants emerged to pull back the long curtain that hung before the entrance to the Grotta Azzurra. The scent of seawater and incense wafted into the room as the major domo hustled the slaves destined for household service out another entrance, keeping himself between the emperor and the youngest procurement. Lannerus eyed Mercurius, but the Prefect stood stock still, the wine cup empty in his hand.

"Swim! Swim!" The emperor shouted and then suppressed a cough.

The newly arrived slaves looked at one another and then through the tunnel, where lithe arms beckoned and a variety of nymphs were prone on rocks or drenched divans, welcoming them into a world that should not exist.

The night had begun.

Lannerus purposely drank more than he cared to and kept away from the ongoing orgy as much as possible, favoring a permanently exhausted but good-humored Egyptian prostitute who was motherly to the young ones and sisterly with her peers. She had long ago sensed his unease with these orchestrated events, much less his occasional role, and always played the part of the jealous harlot, glaring at any of the dripping Ganymedes who surfaced too close to his poolside divan. He relaxed into her arms, and they drank from each other's cups. Anyone not preoccupied, actively fucking or sucking or being sucked, risked being cast in one of the emperor's scripted and increasingly gymnastic sexual dramas. The youngest and most handsome recruits among the Praetorians were always getting pulled into intricate threesomes with the dwarves or circus performers on hand by way of initiation. Lannerus' Egyptian could tell when the night was taking a particularly dark turn. She would theatrically lure him toward one of the more private caves so they could avoid the public trysts starting to populate the grotto. There she would doze in his arms while he nursed the exquisite and ever available Valarian wine that flowed freely within the grotto; it was easily the most expensive and sought-after drink in all of the empire. Tiberius being notoriously parsimonious, Lannerus assumed this was the doing of the major domo; likely his thinking was the more everyone enjoyed and drank the wine, the less they would care about the priapic skeleton floating in a sea of boys before them, laughing and leering, the gigantic ring loose on his boney finger possessing the power to put entire nations to death.

Throughout the night's events, Lannerus observed Tiberius caressing and whispering to the newly procured slaves. The emperor would lower his voice further and exaggeratedly point at Lannerus. The boys would shiver and shrink down into the water. By way of explaining how Lannerus handled certain livestock, the emperor was confirming that his aquatic menagerie were livestock, too.

The next morning's hangover was atrocious, which was exactly what he had hoped for: a mind filled with dark clouds was something he could clean, like a stable, and give him purpose as he exercised through the pain. In the afternoon he focused on the horses, conferred with the men who fed them, brusquely ordered all of the hipposandals be presented for inspection; he caviled over their condition, and issued a slew of mostly unnecessary commands to keep everyone in his orbit moving and fearful of a temper that he only pretended to possess. During the afternoon sexta hora, when everyone retired for to rest during the hottest hour of the day, he sought the shade of the largest tree near the stables and thought of his Egyptian prostitute, wondered if he was too old to reenlist and go off to fight in some foreign war, or that simpering Senator who had long ago offered him the position to oversee his estate at Baiae, he would have had the run of the place. Was that old goat still alive, even? The shadows of the tree's heavy limbs caressed his forehead and he drifted off to sleep only to dream he was drowning, caught underwater by an unseen force that felt like a pair of small hands.

One of the household slaves had fetched him back to the Grotta Azzura to an unexpected scene: yet another batch of "minnows" had been sifted through the nets of empire and deposited onto the shore beneath the Villa Jovis. This lot looked somewhat sickly and malnourished, as if they'd been at sea for quite some time. Some clung together while others tried to disappear into the shadows of the gloomy dark room. Among them, the scullery boy from the day before had been returned to this grouping, all destined for the grotto. Lannerus noted that Mercurius stood about as far from the emperor as he could and decided that his little ploy had been found out. The scullery boy, terrified, held onto one of the bigger young men who bravely stood his ground in the middle of the room, naked, dirty, proud. Taller than the rest, he projected the attitude that his compliance to his captivity was a gift that could just as easily be withdrawn. His fighting spirit was on full display, as was his considerable cock, which was sure to catch the eye of the emperor. Poor boy, Lannerus thought, his energy would be better spent in a provincial coliseum where he could lap up applause. Better than cheeks rouged, bare-bottomed, legs dangling in a pool of tepid sea water, awaiting a wizened and pocked tongue to surface and tug at his member. The scullery boy witnessed Lannerus' eyes on his chosen protector and mistook casual assessment as a threat. He puffed out his weak chest and shot this breaker of horses, a veteran of multiple foreign wars, a look he thought menacing but only made Lannerus chortle. He quickly turned his head least any of the retinue present think he favored the boy, was somehow challenging Mercurius or eying the emperor's property -word would quickly travel to Tiberius and the boy's fate would be sealed: he would be subjected to the most unimaginable sexual humiliations if it were thought he was desired by an other.

Before the festivities could commence, the major domo dutifully recorded their names in his ledger: the former kitchen boy possessed an obscure derivative of Plumo -likely a nickname: *Little Feather*. He shot Lannerus a dirty look as they were escorted out and into the grotto.

A lavish banquet had been assembled within the cavern and a forced sense of merriment pervaded the proceedings. Flamingos had been brought in but were listless and seemed to be failing in the subterranean environs. Lannerus was disappointed and disconcerted that his Egyptian was nowhere to be seen. He hoped she hadn't been assigned other duties within the villa or worse, that the emperor had perceived that he considered her as more a shield than sexual plaything. Mercurius seemed ill at ease and drank more and thus boasted more. None of his comments meant to gain the attention or approval of the emperor gained traction. Tiberius himself seemed in a more deviously sour mood than usual. In mockery of his adopted father and predecessor, Augustus, whose dislike of Tiberius was well known (it was gossiped that he considered the elevation of Tiberius as an opportunity to improve his posthumous reputation, that the-then-future emperor was so surely going to fail as to make the memory of his forerunner that much more lustrous), he wore one of the former emperor's laurel wreaths askance on his grey head. Rather than honor this relic of prior imperial glory, Tiberius often donned it before going for a swim, or while mounting one of the minnows. The laurel was now is great disrepair, nearly leafless, a crooked crown Hades himself would disdain.

After the evening's orgy had commenced in earnest, Lannerus had tried to discretely excuse himself but was barred from leaving by some of the Praetorians who were brought in to help break in the new enlistments. The soldiers took to their task with a mixture of grim amusement and savage abandon, most likely having been deprived of drinking privileges for quite some time to better prepare them for the night's festivities. He lost himself in wine. As the night wore on, and knowing the emperor, while engrossed in his own revery, was observing all, he relieved himself in the mouth of a dwarf to insure he was sufficiently debauched. He roamed the grotto, tried to get the major domo to give him leave through one of the many hidden tunnels, to no avail. He observed the stud, that once and future gladiator, debase himself before a mass of Pretorians, naked save their helmets. Wherever he went, the scullery boy's eyes followed from the farthest edge of the deepest pool, where he tread water continuously in the hopes the emperor would forget about him. Lannerus knew that was an impossibility. And so they were all summoned back into the large receiving cavern, ablaze in hellish torchlight. By prearranged signal, the exhausted, limp form of the scullery boy was raised onto the cleared banquet table. Pretorian guards, nude and engorged, held the youth down by his ankles and wrists. The major domo ceremoniously handed Lannerus his satchel of tools -obviously retrieved from his home by a knowing slave.

While it was technically illegal to castrate a youth for sexual purposes it was so widespread and common that the law in this regard was useless. As eunuchs aged, they were given positions within the household, including food tasters who traveled with the emperor. Many even held positions of power. Mercifully, though he has orchestrated this treacherous affair, Tiberius was not in attendance. Whenever he was, he repeated the same lame joke that Lannerus was his personal vintner. "Here to prune the vines again, are we?" His servants would erupt in laughter as if it were the first time he'd uttered this banality.

Lannerus had observed this sad state of affairs from against the wall of the cave, one hand near a torch as if steadying himself for the work ahead. He kept his hand close to the flame until he could bear it no longer, then moved in and felt the boy's forehead for an inordinate amount of time, to transfer a certain amount of lingering heat.

"He has fever and is too sick to survive the surgery." Lannerus announced, deploying the vocabulary of a doctor rather than the usual coarse words associated with animal husbandry, all the better to drive home his expertise in the matter.

As he turned his back to the boy, the major domo rushed to the side of the stretched and prone figure and felt his brow. Begrudgingly, he nodded his ascent and the boy was hoisted off the table and led away. Lannerus pushed through the now thoroughly drunk Pretorians guarding the cave entrance to take his leave. Laughing, they all covered their exhausted genitals and turned their backs to him.

Lannerus drank cheap wine at a damp tavern with an earthen floor, hoping that the noisy companionship of drunks and prostitutes would distract him from his own racing thoughts, but aside from a few villagers, the place was nearly deserted. No one would talk to him, not even the whores, who looked like they'd seen better days themselves. All seemed to regard him with ill will.

Back in his rooms he tried to sleep but the dreams were

intense and tidal: images of the prone youth, now exaggeratedly writhing before him, beneath him, a giant leering head hovering above the torchlit scene, urging him on; in the dream, he touched the boy's bare bound foot and felt as if struck by lightning -he had once witnessed a horse killed by lightning in Gaul, the sky purple with retribution. Furious thunder, its flesh smoking as it collapsed. He arched his back as memory invaded dream and grappled with his hard cock and the sticky surprise of surfeit seed. He'd not experienced night emissions since a youth in the barracks! Sleep undone, he wiped himself off and stood in the doorway, dawn was straining at the horizon. It was too early to go to the meager baths so he pulled on his tunic and walked to the shore. Best to let the surf cleanse his body and the ocean calm his mind.

Waves crashed again his chest and the colder water below the surface caressed his feet as he watched the sunrise. It had been years since he had gone for a swim in the morning and he was both invigorated and perplexed: he had risked everything to spare a youth he did not know, one who had quickly come to occupy his mind much like a small bird will roost in a tree only to fill it with shimmering song. It was too early to sort these things out so he decided to put everything out of his mind and set himself to spend the day exercising the horses.

Whispers echoed throughout the grotto, disrupted and dispersed by the sound of lapping waves as the tide came in. The majority of the minnows slept the entire day, though there were exceptions, some of the more athletic youth knew that such a life of dispensation led to sallow complexions, thin limbs and bloated bellies, and that their looks and physiques kept them fed and in gold. These young men exercised on the beach every day without fail under the watchful eyes of the guards. As the rocky shore was punctuated with

resilient bush and hidden alcoves, several afternoon trysts occurred between Pretorian and minnow, minnow and minnow, and even guard and guard . . . much salt was returned to the sea though much more was reserved for the nighttime activities.

Further away, the female consorts relieved and refreshed themselves in the surf. Those from other lands taught each other their native language, so they would be able to converse without the Pretorians understanding a word they said. The women who knew magic recognized one another. Among them, they choose from the girls who were brought into the harem the strongest and smartest candidates to induct into their mysteries. While many of them had endured the unendurable, the powers within them were undiminished and the cutlery they had each secreted away at the close of particularly debased banquets were concealed and ready for future use, should the opportunity for escape arise.

Lannerus was beside himself to escape Capri before nightfall. No scenario that he entertained within his wine-soaked mind led anywhere but to his execution. Bribe fisherman who might be in the employ of the emperor? Hiding in one of the abandoned villas meant he would eventually have to risk all to forage for food. How to bring his Egyptian with him? The memory of how her hair had smelled the last time they were together hollowed out his heart. There was no path forward save obedience and he was well aware what dusk would bring.

This time it was the major domo himself who marched across the field, accompanied by two Pretorians, men he did not recognize from the prior evening, meaning Tiberius had refreshed the troops to continue his perverse celebrations.

Torches flared within the confines of the Grotta Azzurra's largest chamber. The emperor was present, as were a select number of his entourage and a number of curious and frightened

92

slaves. A naked Mercurius was spread across the table like a sacrificial bull. The terror in his eyes penetrated Lannerus' soul. Thankfully a leather ball had been strapped into his mouth, though he still whinnied like a foal.

Tiberius was atop one of his portable thrones (he had several and traveled within them, so if caught off guard by the need to hold an audience, he would not be at the mercy of the local trappings. A trick he picked up from Augustus). At his feet was the scullery boy transformed: his costume was that of a Nereid, a loose-fitting viridian toga. Bejeweled bits of coral hung from freshly pierced ears. Bracelets and bangles wrapped his lithe wrists, rewards, no doubt, for services rendered. He regarded Lannerus and the impending proceedings with cool detachment. Lannerus snapped his fingers and the major domo leapt to action: slaves blindfolded the struggling Mercurius and brought down a torch. Lannerus moved with precision and pulled at his victim's plump testicles, least they recede in fear and complicate the procedure. Mercurius bucked wildly as additional soldiers joined to hold him still. Lannerus held his knife to the flame with one hand while pulling Mercurius' penis to the side. He was bemused to see it slightly engorged. Not an uncommon occurrence. He gave the Praetorians at Mercurius' ankles both a nod and they intuited his silent instruction and wrenched the whimpering man's legs farther apart. Lannerus heated the knife as the major domo approached with a bowl of garlic paste. Moving swiftly, he severed the testicles, placing the hot knife against the bloody wound to cauterize the incision and stem the flow of blood. Mercurius went limp, either unconscious from fright and pain or his body relented in full surrender. Lannerus waited the appropriate amount of time, removed the knife and dipped it into the bowl of garlic. He then slathered the paste across the blackened wound to further guard against infection. A stooped kitchen slave snuck into the room and silently removed the severed testicles. Lannerus understood from prior banquets that these fleshy orbs would be cooked and served as a special course to their prior owner.

All for the emperor's amusement.

Lannerus examined his work. All in all, a good gelding.

"He needs to rest." He wiped the still warm blade against his thigh and entered the grotto for a refreshing dip.

The minnows all fastidiously avoided him, swimming away or leaping out of the pool. He took a deep breath, closed his eyes and submerged into the dark waters. Dreams, fears, hopes, all swirled within his mind. He surfaced, craving wine. His Egyptian, naked, was entering the water with a smile. He swam to meet her.

Between the torches on the farthest wall hung an ancient Greek mask. Eyeless, it allowed Tiberius to observe the grotto from a secret passage. Lannerus perceived a flicker of movement, and knowing that Tiberius was busy fawning over his new favorite, guessed it was the young Caligula. Favored by the soldiers, the emperor's adoptive nephew and heir apparent was recurrently described as Tiberius' opposite: moral, chaste, a beacon of hope for an empire battered and bruised by cruelty and unrelenting decades of vice.

The world will enter a new, bright era when Caligula dons the purple, Lannerus thought, *and none too soon.*

Hypoxyphilia

My throat is like a fist. Maybe it's more the wrist, that root of power and dexterity that grows into the hand. The hand on my throat. Something of an Ouroboros? Looping, headless, swallowing itself in a blind clasp? I imagine a wristwatch on a veiny arm impossibly bent in on itself, an eyeless lock of two hands growing out of one another.

I must be running out of oxygen, so I tap out.

He's heavy atop me, crushing my penis into a flaccid conduit of building tension and old laments. Sweaty hand on the taunt thigh of my unnamed partner, a wispy tap, what he must think is a caress, a bit of urging onward, to keep choking me. But that's not what I want (it's completely and utterly what I want, to be pushed to the edge of need and now I need air. I must breathe. I must surface, having so luxuriated at the silty bottom of consciousness.) but he doesn't heed my call and so I scratch, thinking the bite of my nails will elicit attention and that elicits only anger and a tighter squeeze and really, I'm all out of options, aren't I? I mean, I have no voice in this situation, do I? One of the few blessed moments where I am unable to express myself, bark an order, exude a sigh, all of that is taken by the hand on my throat.

Choking, I wish I could swallow and find it ironic that this man's incidental drool has whetted my lips.

I quit slapping his thighs and grip the mattress as his cock knocks about in my ass. His back arches and his legs go straight and I can tell he's cumming and once again I don't feel any internal piercing, what my friend Jeffrey calls "hot arrows" –he loves it when men cum inside him, exalts in it, exclaims he can feel the threads lance his hollows and yet I feel nothing but relief as the weight crashing down on my abdomen and torso heralds the liberation of the hand from my throat -that which unties all that binds my tense body and fractured mind and an exquisite orgasm is released: a flock of skittish birds that scatter, shattering my shoulders to fly out of my upturned chin as I shoot but not this time. This time my unnamed guest, via Adam4Adam, kicking off his shoes as I shut the door, mouth open, looking past me, already fixated on the promised mount and rut, of my texted assurance that my body was his to abuse. Now he forgets to let go and so I go black around the eyes again, the narrowing of vision, the wings of said birds reaching toward each other instead of the sky and with frayed feathers the light shrinks and I feel bad that I didn't pay the rent yet, that there is a week's worth of unopened mail on the dining room table, that I forgot to text Jeffrey a picture of my trick and the promise to call while the cum is cooling in my cavity, a glass of red wine in hand as I relive every detail over the phone. (He always returns the favor. Our adventures the same but different. He hunts in parks and midnight parking garages, so I get text messages of census and locale that, if read aloud, sound as if delivered by the disembodied narrator of a weird nature show: "Park mostly empty. Winter means no leaves, so no cover. Four guys fighting over one top. I'm horny but willing to wait. It is cold but more guys will appear after bars close." Though I never get pictures, once he accidentally called me on his cell phone while in the middle of a fuck and I could hear their noises, the rummaging around in one another's bodies like bears rooting through tipped over trashcans.)

I gasp.

Lost in the heady swirl of his own spent ecstasy, this man doesn't get it, that his hand on my throat will accidentally erase my soul. Then he shifts and instinctively I suck in air and my erection swells and with a cough I excrete jagged bursts of semen and he looks at me quizzically, as if I were somehow overacting.

He rises in one bound and struggles to pull his pants on. Though I drew the shades some late afternoon sun slips in and glints off his silver wristwatch.

Stretching and shaking on the bed, sheets long ago pushed down by desperate legs, two drowning men trying to gain traction in the sea of each other, I clench my hands. My palms open like a flower, the flower of a fist that holds a secret only someone else can release, tease out of me, a truth that needs another to be heard.

My fist is like a throat.

Bent on Midnight Frolic

1971. T-Bone, 23, Hispanic, 5'4", 180 lbs., 7.5 inches, uncircumcised.

T-Bone stood on the cusp of the dark wooded path and reflexively cracked his knuckles and rolled his head back and forth, his thick neck corded and strong (like a T-bone, hence the nickname). He was buzzed, having chugged several beers in a row and didn't know how he knew about the Ramble, probably guys joking in the halls at Saint Barnabas High School. Since he'd started working in Manhattan as a bouncer, queers certainly checked him out *a lot*. He mostly ignored them, even the one who had an ass like a woman's –and he was definitely an ass man, but lately, when the two fags who worked coat check looked him up and down, his cock twitched and, in the deeper waters of his mind, memories of summers at his cousin's house – Fruit of the Loom underwear off and flashlights on – flickered like the silver tails of an ancient Coelacanth, primeval but very much alive and moving through the darkest of currents.

The quiet unnerved him as he rocked back and forth on his heels and, sensing that someone was coming up slowly behind him, he took the plunge. The woods were wild. Men in groups or solo, the stench of weed, half-hearted whispering and the occasional "O' baby, please" –a shocking echo to his pleas to Carmen, one that made him feel that he'd stepped through the looking glass and all these other men were mere reflections of his lust. It was perfectly okay and natural to reach through the mirror and touch an extension of yourself. A group of Boricuas stood close together talking low, arms heavy across one another's shoulders, distended wife beater shirts showing muscled backs and juvenile tattoos –he spun away in the other direction. *What if they were from the barrio?* The tumescence in his jeans demanded attention. He kept cupping his package and looking about, unsure of how to engage but knowing that it was only moments away –a doe-like golden haired boy stepped into the path and froze. His beauty was luminal. A throat so thin, even in the weak moonlight, T-Bone noticed a slow swallow of anticipation. He walked up fast and close and the young man extended his neck downward in surrender. Lips parted, lithe arms out, he wore nothing but lose cutoff jean shorts. T-Bone put his thick fingers on the boy's slender neck and pushed him down.

"Ay, Dios mìo."

If he hadn't been drunk – drunk on need, not beer – he might have noticed that, even though his eyes were closed, there was a nimbus of golden light around the head bobbing between his thighs.

1947. *Marcus Seymour Marigold, 27, Caucasian, 5'6", 125 lbs., 9 inches, circumcised.*

Marcus slipped into Central Park on his way to work in the Brill Building. His short commute from a cold water flat on East 53rd made mornings a leisurely treat: a stroll, then breakfast at one of the automats in Times Square. Friends (tricks where the sex petered out but they still caught up in bars –guys were always shocked, once they'd drifted into acquaintances, that Marcus always gave his real name) were impressed that he worked in the Brill Building. Though he wasn't in the music industry, he brushed shoulders with stars nearly every week and told stories out of turn about who had pulled out the longest member at the urinals. He had read that morning in the Times that the Dutch had donated a swath of tulips, gratitude for the United States war efforts, to be planted in Central Park.

It was a chilly April morning, the kind of day where the temperature rose rapidly –the frost on the marble statues turned from silvery verdigris into runny dew before noon. Secretaries stalked into the subway with their coats tucked between their arms, scarves stuffed in purses. Men forgot their hats on their desks. He knew from the newspaper article that the tulips were to be planted in a neat square near that portion of the park called the Ramble. He'd been there, of course, but had always struck out. Fearful that the man approaching was a policeman, he'd resorted to picking up obvious trade in Bryant Park. However, after wandering the park for half an hour, he was on the verge of disappointment when the trail twisted into a square of dark, tilled soil: no green shoots, just subterranean hard bulbs of colorful flower about to burst into living fireworks, announcing, with Stravinsky-like fanfare, the arrival of spring. Standing still, he breathed in the crisp air and observed a twittering squirrel scuttle down the long branch of a winter hardened Ginkgo tree. Marcus decided that he would alter his morning stroll and mark this spot every morning, to observe the birth of the tulips, to watch a season unfold. More than once, he'd wished he owned a camera, knew how to take good pictures. But he was also secretly pleased that some moments go forever unrecorded, that the private discourses of dawn were his alone.

For the duration of spring, Marcus revisited this little field to observe their progress and growth. Year after year the tulips were replanted, once more in Central Park before being moved to the long median that divided Park Avenue. He always made an appreciative effort to pause and note the progress of the blooms. Yet those mornings of the initial planting within the park were somehow significant to him. He could be forgiven for not noticing in the morning light that one flower, the last bulb to bloom, pulsed with a golden hue.

1983. *James Garamond, 27, Caucasian, 5'8", 145 lbs., 5.5 inches, circumcised.*

James had heard rumors about the "Golden Boy of the Ramble," had indeed thought he'd caught a glimpse of his gossamer form once, slipping off a large rock to follow a rather rough-looking gentleman. He'd seen a hot blond at the Continental Baths last summer that had a certain air about him, having dispensed with the prerequisite towel and seemingly floated through the halls. James was on Quaaludes that particular night and assumed the guy was just European, but now, having heard more than one ribald tale in the bars, stories swapped down by the trucks at midnight near the piers, he couldn't help but wonder if this boy was some sexual fantasy writ large: a cipher on which the community's collective lust was projected. Christopher Street Magazine had recently accepted some of his articles, had asked for more –the New York Times had rejected a review of the new Edmund White novel, but encouragingly so. Tonight, he felt like he was on the trail of a real story, something different that would help prove his chops *and* get him noticed.

The night air had cooled. The dampness of the soil intermingling with spilt beer and semen generated a primal stench interrupted by stale cigarette smoke and the quiet exhalations of enraptured men. A shirtless black youth in bright red jogging shorts whisked pass and, from out of the darkness, a pale white arm reached to stroke the moving quarry but failed to connect. The pale limb went slack and James caught his breath

–he'd had no idea someone else was so close. He instinctively patted his wallet. It was a dummy, stuffed with a few singles and crumpled receipts so any mugger would think it was legit –he'd been mugged a few times crossing the park at night so now he kept his license and a folded twenty tucked into his tight tube socks, though he regretted wearing his new Reeboks as the trampled ground was muddy and trash-strewn. Another man in cut-offs sauntered past, a handkerchief in his back pocket. *So seventies*, James silently sniggered, but he pursued, not out of any sexual interest, but to keep moving. Winding his way down one of the dim paths, he spied two men talking close, sharing a joint, one with his cock out, long, limp and damp as if recently sucked, now cooling off in the night air. In the city two years, he still reeled, still marveled, at how different life was here than in his hometown of Indianapolis. There cruising was circumspect, hesitant, fearful. In New York it was flagrant sport, feral and above all else, constant. Not too far from the weak light and mosquito whirl of the rare working street lamp, the silhouette of men encircling each other, the quiet grunts and rhythmic sawing of elbows pulled at him. Forgetting his "research," James pulled off his shirt, fingered his hairy chest and looked for a break in the action so he could join. At the other end of the sexual circus he heard a wizened cough as a man was roughly pushed out. He was wild-eyed, high or drunk or both, he held his wrinkled shirt to his mouth to stifle his coughing –still, such ostracism was rare. James had been amused that though only hot guys approached other hot guys at the bars; anything went in the Ramble. Here he'd witnessed couplings so out of proportion in terms of expectations and assumptions that they ran from the humorous to the touching. But this guy seemed beyond deranged, on drugs and forcing himself on the group. Trying to use his exit as a point of entry, James ducked between a pair of naked, grappling men and noticed that, as they passed, the coughing man's back was riddled with dark crusty spots. James froze. Just a few days ago, he was at the gym and caught sight of a young man he'd tricked with a few months ago changing in the locker room. He rather self-consciously pulled his collar up to conceal a purplish bruise, what James had thought was the thumbprint of a rather severe hickey at the time. Now he wasn't so sure. His sexual appetite dissipated. James disengaged from the group and left the park and headed to Cat's Bar for a drink. Gossip about the Golden Boy of the Ramble all but ceased after an article about a new "gay cancer" appeared later that month in the Times.

James will have plenty else to write about.

1988. *Golden Boy. Age unknown, fluctuating height, between 5'4" and 6'2", depending on the length of the summer, same with his weight and cock size, uncircumcised (naturally).*

Golden Boy. He'd heard that he was called that for several seasons and then no more. Curious that a name had been assigned to him, unconcerned that it was forgotten, he felt the absence of the men from before. It was as if they had been folded up and put away further into the darkness of the park, the black spaces of the city, the cold forgetful lake between the stars. Their lights had gone out and he missed them, whimpered even, when one that he had known so closely, had tasted deeply, just snapped out of existence. No matter how far away, how quickly that light had extinguished or painfully lingered, he knew when they were gone. Others stepped in to feed him, to take him and take from him, but differently, with a more abrasive economy than before, with condoms, with whiskey and fear on their breath. Everything had changed but the longing.

He learned bits of the language of men, enough to say to himself "*I am not gold. I am green. I am not a boy, I am hungry.*" And though he drank from an endless fountain of semen most nights (except when it rained, except when it snowed), and as men bent him over and pushed his face down until he ate the blackest dirt and the insects secreted within, he was still ravenous. Some men pushed him to his knees and fucked his mouth until his bruised lips bled. Others laughed ruefully while urinating on his hair. Some fucked him slowly, lovingly, with all the deliberation of a secret dance, so that he was as still for them as a firm oak, their hands clasping his perfect waist as they unburdened themselves within his hot cavity. They whispered to him in every language, thick tongues in his ear. Some smelled like hard work, some like cheap wine and tooth decay, others a hint of their wives' perfume or too many nights sleeping rough on benches. He took from them all and still hungered.

1988. *Jonathan C. Raleigh, 45, Caucasian, 6'1", 185, 6 inches, uncircumcised.*

Raleigh (all his friends, even his wife, called him Raleigh) loved his business trips to New York City. He hated the Javitz Center, loudly, repeatedly disclaiming to anyone in earshot, "It's like an airport without a city, for Christ sakes," as if that joke never got old. As a buyer for a major chain of department stores across the South, he carried a lot of weight and was deservedly wined and dined during his quarterly visits to the Big Apple. He told stories that were too long, referencing his wife so often that more than one designer had rolled their eyes, mouthing "Methinks he doth protest too much." Raleigh eschewed the baths and bars during the spring and summer months and made sure he always booked the Marriot in Times Square. He would tell his wife he'd call her in the morning —that he'd be with sellers all night, no matter how often she insisted that he call her when he got in, that there were Puerto Ricans everywhere. (She'd latched onto that particular group as the cause of all malfeasance in New York City for no other reason than that they'd recently befriended a black couple at church, so for her it was like moving to a different city and having to root for a new team.)

Raleigh lit a Benson and Hedges, dropped the match and stepped into the Ramble. It was a warm night and men in shorts promenaded past. Men and boys – young swishy things, cadet cocksuckers, he thought – new arrivals to the woods: their nascent sexual energy was as prominent as the humidity, as constant as the buzz of invisible crickets punctuated by the grunts of rutting men. He pawed his impatient erection, heavy in his linen trousers. He kept his suit and tie on when entering the Ramble –as he'd aged, he had observed that certain men were attracted to business attire and willing to enter into some pretty hot scenes. A naked man with long hair stepped from behind a black tree and straddled the trunk, one hand ridiculously caressing the bark. Raleigh moved on. Now freely perspiring, he took a handkerchief from his pocket and patted his brow. As he crammed it back into his pocket, he realized that he'd forgotten to take off his wedding ring. He had heard horror stories about muggings in Central Park and had always left it in the hotel safe before venturing out, but tonight he had come directly from the bar, fueled by too many Chivas on the rocks. His cheeks reddened with annoyance. He didn't dare take the ring off and slip it into his pocket –it was too dark, the action too suspicious. A gaggle of ghetto youth burst laughing from the bushes and his hand instinctively dropped to his rear, as if to protect his precious wallet, but their peals of laughter bloomed into effeminate whispers so he relaxed. But it was time to get on with it.

Golden Boy arched his back and opened his mouth wide –his extended tongue pulling moisture from the air. He was wearing a pair of torn, soiled madras shorts he'd found the other morning draped across the back of a park bench. And nothing else. Broken glass didn't puncture his bare feet; the rough boulders that dotted the Ramble never scraped his backside. He'd been entered by several men already tonight, and had been on his knees pleasing a group at the edge of the Central Park Lake for quite some time, the stoic twin cameo of the Dakota apartment building peering over the Park's edge like disapproving neighbors. He didn't mark time as the men who frequented the park did. He tasted seasons. Hibernating winters within the trunk of the largest tree he could secret himself within, he would stretch himself into a long line of golden sap and wait until the first birdsong of spring, then at dusk he pulled his thin, naked body from out of the tree and thank his host with a deep, reverent bow before making his way through the paths of the Ramble, returning at dawn to sleep away the day. As spring turned to summer, he grew stronger and taller, repeating the hot whispers men dripped into his ear until the words became something he could use though he wasn't aware that different languages existed, so when he did speak it was an odd mixture of Spanish and English. (He had heard dozens of languages but those two were the most frequently spoken as cocks slipped in and out of him.) He retained these words while he slept through the winter. As he logged more and more winters, he thought more about his hunger and the men who came to him in the park. He fed from their beings, enjoying their fluids and heat, but was this what he was meant to do? And the confines of existence, the stone walls he never crossed, what kept him contained —was he rooted here like the trees? Questions like these arose if he went too long without touching a man and before the answers could come a man always did.

He heard the promise of an unzipped fly and blinked as a broad-shouldered man stood before him, legs wide apart. Golden Boy slinked down onto his knees and fed. When he was done, as always, he wanted more.

Raleigh pulled his cock out of his pants while watching a nearly naked young man service a construction worker. Once again, he was in awe of the secret fraternity to which he had been inducted. When he first read that Life Magazine article on San Francisco as a teen, he'd felt repulsed. He had never had a desire to be "gay" or leave his wife –he loved her, he loved their Atlanta, two-car garage home together. But what he had done with one of the other guys on the wrestling team remained: it was something that had brightened in his mind where he had always been led to believe that it would fade. So year after year he came here to enact that same desire, but for him these were still only moments, a vice, not a "life style."

As the construction worker stepped away, Raleigh eagerly stepped up, ready to unload, to be done with it and back in his hotel room in time to watch Carson. Young lips brushed his cock and he shuddered and thought of the slender Pan Am attendant who'd refreshed his drink on the flight over, paid him just enough extra attention that he knew, they both knew, and as he engorged across nimble tongue he wondered what it would be like to take someone in his hotel room bed instead –the thought of the unanswered phone ringing, tanned legs spread on clean sheets. He was about to cum and jammed his fingers into the hot mouth beneath him to take total control and Golden Boy turned his head as if he had been in a desert for years, since his floral birth, and had never taken a drink before. Golden Boy lit up like a new sun and fear gripped Raleigh's spine as he thought this new light emanated from the beam of a policeman's flashlight, that he was about to be arrested. His boss would be woken up by the phone call, still in bed, listening in silence as gleeful Yankees explained that his employee had been caught with his penis inserted in another man's mouth and would he like to arrange bail via Western Union?

Golden Boy's eyes were open wide and he sucked harder than he'd ever sucked before as his true need churned within the pit of his stomach: he tasted gold for the first time, sumptuous ore, something that he innately knew he was meant to burrow through the earth and find and covet but somehow his path had been diverted by this sticky river of salt. He glowed even brighter and Raleigh, seized by panic, tried to extract himself from this teething, fiery starling by planting one foot on the boy's shoulder while yanking his hand free. Golden Boy couldn't let this prize go so he bit down hard and blood filled his mouth —another new taste, not bad but nowhere near as nutritious as the wedding band that rolled across his tongue. His teeth sharpened and worked the finger quickly away from the screaming man's hand. Golden Boy had nightly lapped up semen, occasionally drank urine – once a disappointed man shoved a stick roughly up his ass (disappointed because Golden Boy didn't scream but widened his slippery hole to be more accommodating) – and now tasted blood. None of which had prepared him for the flavors of gold. His skin practically burned. For the first time his wavering erection was sincere and not mere mimicry of those around him. Golden Boy swallowed the metallic morsel and dropped to the ground, purring in ecstasy.

Raleigh ran through the woods silently, holding his bleeding hand up as if it were something disgusting that he'd like to throw away but was nevertheless responsible for. He stifled a whimper, fearful that sounding like a wounded animal would attract other humanoid carnivores to take his wallet, strip him naked, and beat him to death. He tried not to hyperventilate as he reached 5th Avenue and hailed a cab.

In his hotel room, injured hand deep in a silvery ice bucket as the water turned pink, desperation ran its course and Raleigh called the concierge and requested an ambulance. There was no way he could explain away *this* one. (Honey, he's a Jehovah's Witness who was just so dehydrated I *had* to invite him in for a glass of water. I'm not sure how his jock strap ended up on the bathroom floor. They have mighty strange rites, like Mormons, you know?) He took yet another aspirin and chased it with one of those little plastic bottles of Captain Morgan's rum the airline steward and flirtatiously dropped in his lap. He wasn't going to call his wife tonight or tomorrow. Or his boss. He wasn't going home. There was terse knocking at the hotel room door but he was too woozy to answer. Raleigh needed a long nap. Maybe he could get a job at Macy's. Keys rattled and someone let themselves into the room saying, "Sir, sir? Are you alright?" He didn't bother to answer. The throbbing pain coursing up his arm felt permanent. And if winters were too hard here, he thought drily, he could always move to San Francisco.

1992. *Marcus Seymour Marigold, 72, Caucasian, 5'6", 142 lbs., 9 inches, circumcised.*

Snickles Two's tail twitched as she sensed an unseen squirrel. Marcus was patient and let the Pomeranian work her excitement out before giving the leash a gentle tug. Retired for the better part of a decade, he was still surprised at how his routine was similar to his former work day, albeit with more naps, neighbors were now friends instead of strangers, and the wine bottle was opened earlier and earlier. Same apartment as when he moved to the city, the five-floor walk-up kept him lean. People often thought he was at least ten years younger than his actual age. Snickles Two whined and pulled him in a new direction and he let himself be led deeper into the park.

Though the sun had not yet set, Golden Boy slipped out from within the folds of an oak tree and sat on the water's edge. He wore a tight black t shirt and a pair of faded gym shorts that he's salvaged from the trash. Fingers lazing in the water, a small dog nuzzled him from behind. He turned to see an apologetic older man tugging at the leash and Golden Boy laughed.

"It's okay. I am here to make new friends."

Marcus puzzled at the stilted accent and let Snickles Two off her leash. She bound and twirled over her new found freedom and the youth who so attracted her rolled in the dirt, matching the dog's enthusiasm with an almost alarming alacrity. He was dumbstruck by how attractive the young man was —a halo of sexual energy emanated from around his sinewy body like a barely perceptible fog. Now squatting and petting the dog, Golden Boy felt Marcus staring at him, his mouth literally open in wonderment, so he stretched and stood and took off his shirt. Marcus looked around to see if this was really happening and ran through the mental list of possibilities:

This kid is crazy.
He's a weird foreigner.
He's a scam artist.
He's homeless.
Maybe he's into older guys.
This kid is crazy.
He's on drugs.
If he wants a Daddy, my Social Security check wasn't made

for two.

This kid is a homeless, crazy, weird foreign scam artist on drugs.

Maybe he just likes me?

…

A tourist family briskly wheeled a stroller between them.

Golden Boy mouthed "What do you want?"

Marcus swallowed and whispered "For you to come home with me."

Golden Boy had shaped himself to every fantasy placed before him, had ever and always acquiesced, so he simply nodded in agreement. Snickles Two sensed the new bond and approved in a frenzy of slobber and tail wagging. Marcus smiled weakly, alternate strings of hope and fear laced his heart so tightly that he couldn't speak, so instead he offered his arm and Golden Boy took it. Snickles Two launched them homeward and shortly Golden Boy stepped out of the park for the first time.

Locking the door behind them, Marcus was shocked when they made it inside his apartment –he hadn't entertained male company since Clifford, already wasting away from AIDS, had died of pneumonia in the early eighties. He was shocked that he was making tea for two, that Snickles Two so obviously approved, that the boy lounging on his couch seemed so preternaturally peaceful and at ease in his home. That he had walked barefoot in the streets of Manhattan, that alternately crossing his long legs revealed the soles of his feet to be perfectly clean was another matter altogether. There was much to ponder and ask and yet he just wanted to sit with this boy and bask in his youthful radiance. Still, there were enough red flags that he also thought to alert one of his closer friends in the building that he had a guest, to check up on him in a little while but then Golden Boy stood and slipped out of his shorts and opened his arms and Marcus went to him. The tea pot whistled and they pulled apart long enough to turn off the stove, put Snickles Two in the kitchen with some hastily poured dog food and then they stumbled and tugged at one another into the bed room. Marcus whispered into his ear and Golden Boy smiled –happy to hear some nearly forgotten words from seasons past.

Because Marcus never asked Golden Boy to leave, he stayed. He would sleep most of the day, which initially vexed the older man. Whenever he would walk the dog or run his errands, he was suspicious upon his return the boy would be gone, that his apartment would be robbed. But he got used to the strange youth in his bed always being there. Strange because if Marcus came home late, or was out during the evenings, whenever he returned he often found the boy naked in bed, legs spread with a vibrant oozing erection while he teethed on one of the pewter candlesticks his mother had left him. Strange because he never asked for anything, never called friends, never made requests, demands, trouble, never argued, preferred to be as nearly naked as possible indoors or out, and though he occasionally used a Spanish word or two, never gave a hint to his background.

Some of his friends were bemused, some outraged, some pitied him until they met Golden Boy, whom he introduced as "Goldie," and then quite a few were jealous. His downstairs neighbor, Marcie, who, like Marcus was retired but thought leaving New York was not only ridiculous but paramount to a death sentence, threatened to call the police and took every opportunity to question Goldie. Marcie had gone to meet Marcus at the hospital the night Clifford had passed. She sat with him quietly in the cab home as it was stuck in traffic. She passed a twenty-dollar bill to the driver and touched Marcus on the knee and said, "Come." He followed and they walked the rest of the way home together. He wept openly as they made their way down Lexington and she said nothing. Marcie understood grief as a bodily force, a series of breath-driven upheavals –the violent spin of a dropped compass. She knew this was coming and had a bottle of whiskey ready, standing guard under the sink with the Lysol. They've been friends now for twenty-five years. Her reservations about Goldie were never completely laid to rest but she liked that he would run errands for the older residents of the building. His inability to learn how to play bridge confirmed her suspicion that he was probably "simple" –her word, to the point where she worried over who would look after Goldie once Marcus was gone.

One afternoon Marcus was clearing out his dresser to take some old clothes to a charity re-sale shop when he noticed that his gold cufflinks were missing. A sigh of relief passed his lips. He'd fretted for the better part of the year that this perfect body on his couch was too good to be true. He relished the fight they were going to have, when Goldie came home from walking Snickles Two, the admonishments, the confession (and that the boy would finally drop that weird accent), the intense make-up sex –he needed them to finally get to a place of truth. He heard the keys at the lock and the jangle of Snickles Two's collar and as the door opened Marcus was positioned dramatically, square in the middle of the living room, mouth drawn –the empty velvet box that had held cufflinks in his palm open wide like the maw of a tattling child.

Golden Boy smiled as Snickles Two danced between Marcus' legs and then made for the water bowl. Marcus stood still as the boy followed the dog into the kitchen. He resolved to stand there until he received an honest response, tears welling in his eyes, tears of regret as he was terrified of losing him, that the price of his accusation would be an empty bed. His Goldie quickly returned, now shirtless (he was forever shedding clothes the minute he came home) and holding a spoon. Marcus recognized it as a piece of the good silver he hadn't taken out in probably a decade. He wearily committed to counting them after whatever fight they were about to have blew over, but the thought dissipated as the boy solemnly nodded toward his upraised palm in acknowledgement over the missing cufflinks and placed the spoon in his mouth and closed his eyes. His body seemed to vibrate like a tuning fork and he fell to his knees. Marcus dropped the empty velvet box and rushed to his side. The boy sighed and opened his mouth and the melting end of the spoon dropped and sizzled into the carpet. The boy twitched in ecstasy, one finger on his erect pink nipple, a wild erection straining against his shorts. Marcus wept. He cried knowing that, having craved an answer, all he could afford was more mystery, and that now he would have to pay for it with silver and gold.

After the incident on the carpet, far from counting the silverware, Marcus put what remained of his family heirloom under the bed. After a few weeks, when the cypress box was depleted, Marcus would buy cufflinks and metal trinkets at the neighborhood thrift shops, feeding his ravenous boy on the couch or in bed, sometimes on the floor. The feedings were always carnal affairs. When Marcus first inserted a tacky serving spoon into his ass, Golden Boy's moans of ecstasy drove the older man wild. Upon closer inspection he found the expansive, needy nature of the boy's hypnotic hole an addictive necessity.

Marcus masturbated daily with his face between raised legs slipping objects inside and watching them dissolve as Golden Boy shook back and forth. Ignored, Snickles Two would whine and shit on the kitchen floor. Marcie, tired of knocking, would slip snide notes under his door, and questioned the other neighbors about Marcus' increasingly bizarre, aloof behavior, and if anyone else had lent him unreturned kitchen utensils.

When social services arrived, the apartment was a fetid mess, the air thick with the stench of dog shit, semen, and moldering Chinese food. Marcus, looking pale and wane wouldn't let them in. One day, as Goldie took Snickles Two for a rare walk, Marcie slipped into the apartment before Marcus had time to close the door. She was appalled at the stench and disarray.

"Oh Marcus, Clifford would be so ashamed."

She played her strongest card and was shocked when he blinked –he in was in his boxers, a dirty blanket across his shoulders, his eyes unfocused and hollow –he looked unsure of just who she was talking about.

"Let's go to my place, I'll make some coffee and we can talk about this." She gestured at the trash-strewn floor, barely able to hide the contempt in her voice.

"Okay, Marcie, I'd like that." He sounded so defeated, so weak. She was taken aback, so sure of his refusal that she hadn't actually planned how to talk some sense into him. He wavered, looking confused, so she grabbed him by the elbow and silently prayed that the new couple across the hall from her was home –one of them was a nurse and might able to help. As they took the steps one by one, Snickles Two came bounding up the stairwell, his loose leash flogging the steps behind him. Marcus rubbed his eyes and called out "Goldie, Goldie!" and then collapsed weeping as Marcie ran down to the next floor and started banging on the nearest apartment door.

1999, *Daniel Elon, 33, Jewish, 5'6", 146 lbs., 7 inches, circumcised.*

A native New Yorker, Daniel was annoyed that he was lost in the park. His wife and their friends were close by, lounging on the picnic blanket enjoying the last of the summer's symphonies while he had gotten turned around after excusing himself to take a leak. Occasionally he could hear snippets of music as he turned a corner. There were men everywhere, hushed men cruising –he was surprised that this activity still went on in the age of AIDS. But as a doctor, and specifically an internist, he knew better than to discriminate –after all, his cousin Gage had died of the disease. Still, he shuddered that gay men still took such unnecessary risks.

Humidity permeated the August heat –it hung off the trees like thick moss. Parched and inebriated, Daniel just wanted out, yet he had drunk more than his share of wine and the urge to urinate again was overwhelming. (This always happened when he was under stress.) He secreted himself between two dusty boulders and undid his fly. He could feel unseen eyes and let his chinos drop a bit more to reveal the hairy cleave of his ass. Sweat pearled at his ear as he let loose a torrent of piss against the nearest tree trunk. He'd always been particularly proud of his penis; in college and now at the gym, he liked to be naked and seen by other men. He felt as if he were single handedly dispelling the myth that Jewish men had small pricks, and relished the fact that his thick cock was as long soft as it was hard. He arched his back and stretched out his arms as his dick lengthened, a droplet of urine that had caught in his now retracted foreskin glistened in the moonlight.

He moved his hips back and forth; ostensibly to shake out any remaining drops of piss, but also anyone around would better to see the silhouette of his cock come alive. His pants dropped to his ankles as he began to stroke himself. Another pair of hands joined in, one on his cock, the other clutched his furry abdomen. Daniel gasped and relaxed as the quickening grip brought him closer to orgasm; hot breath on his ear –nimble tongue swabbed the sweat across the nape of his neck like a darting humming bird. The hands gathering his flesh were young, practically incandescent. He turned his head to get a better look at who was jacking him off when lips met his. *Oh, he thought I was turning around to kiss him–well HIV doesn't transmit easily through saliva, so there isn't much of a risk –I need to get back to Sheila –Oh God that feels good–*

Daniel groped and turned, a web of pre-cum from both their hard cocks further linking their bodies. The youth kissed him deeply and Daniel gasped as the kiss turned more urgent, probing, the tongue in his mouth fraught, expansive. Sharp pain gripped his skull. He struggled, caught between the tree trunk and the constricting grip around his waist. He gagged as the muscle pushing through his mouth rhythmically worked out one gold filling after another. He hit his attacker, who just held him tighter. They were now face to face: he was a mere boy(!), his eyes off in the distance as Daniel's erection flagged and blood pooled in his mouth to such a degree that he gulped it down or risked choking and no one came to his aid as no one could hear him for the boy also ate his screams.

1947. *Bjorn, 19, Caucasian, 5'5", 135 lbs., 4.5 inches, uncircumcised.*

The shed stank of moist, wormy compost. Still, he welcomed the bit of warmth trapped beneath the corrugated tin roof arching over row after row of tulip bulbs. He and his boss, Sem, had arrived at the same time —the crack of dawn, and both drank coffee from their oddly matching thermoses in silence. Bjorn had recently graduated from Agriculture College and looked after the plants as if he were running an orphanage: his delicate charges unlikely to live through the night without his solemn care. The much older Sem was gruff and quiet. He'd been imprisoned for black marketeering during the war, and whatever had happened to him at the camp had left scars that ran deep. As a supervisor, he was cautious and calm, though he could crack a grin after a few pints of lager. Whenever Bjorn finished his cigarette and flicked the butt, he always felt Sem greedily tracking its progress, as if later, if another war broke out and rations ran thin, he'd know where to go to salvage a few remaining wisps of tobacco.

A farmer drove up in a flatbed heavy with grim soil. The driver didn't get out so Sem jogged over, whispered harshly through the barely rolled down window, and shoved some money into the crack. He motioned for Bjorn who nodded and grabbed a shovel. He knew from the first shovelful that the consistency of the dirt was too fine, that it was leavened with ash. They shoveled in silence and when they were done the farmer drove off. The sky brightened but Bjorn could smell a burnt, powdery stench. Times were hard. There were still so little livestock in the Netherlands that fertilizer was expensive; they had to make do. During moonless nights, poor farmers would dig up the black sooty earth surrounding the dismantled concentration camp. He knew the valley where it had been, was told by his parents in hushed tones that the camp there was much worse than the simple way station everyone had been led to believe. It was rumored that all of the inverts and transvestites of Rotterdam were brought there and, unlike Sem, never left. Better was when he was a child and his grandparents told him ancient bedtime stories about the fey folk of the valley, stories of elves and sprites hungry for hidden treasure. These were wonderful tales of mischievous creatures bent on midnight frolic. He wondered if such fables were meant to die with their generation, for the valley was now poisoned by unspoken cruelty and torture. No matter how quickly they pulled down the barbed wire, the very dirt, the essence from which all else was meant to grow, was tainted.

Sem went to check on the water pump as Bjorn pushed a wheelbarrow of black earth into the shed. He scooped up the soil and patted it gingerly around each bulb. He shook out clumps of old root –*the farmers must have been digging deeper*, he thought as he carefully molded the dirt around the nascent bulbs. A primeval bit of seed, of *something* hard, dropped into the planter and Bjorn absently patted it into the soil surrounding a rather sturdy bulb. It was older than the tales Bjorn's grandparents told him, from before the Netherlands had their kings, certainly well before men gained the sophisticated skills with which to engineer ovens hot enough to turn other men into ash.

Bjorn was proud that the current crop of tulips was destined for New York City. The Netherlands were gifting thousands of bulbs to the U.S. in gratitude for their monumental help during and after the war. The gesture was wonderful but, really, the government was buying up the tulips to spur the economy. He hoped the New World had an early spring, to give the flowers their fullest bloom.

2017. *Call him whatever the fuck you want just don't call him Golden Boy. Eternal, A color you can't see, 6', 125, lbs., 10.5*

inches, uncircumcised (naturally).

He's not golden. He is the root and the leaf and the yearning sap that links and loops between the men who nightly come to the park, fellow vessels waiting to fill or be filled. How they shudder and gasp as he works them open. Many grunt and push off him and stumble out of the brush, buckle knocking knuckle. Few, a sacrosanct few, his whimpering choir of the chosen few —they stay and surrender and nestle down into the dirt, one cheek flat in a puddle, eyes reaching back like desperate hands trying to grab the steering wheel of a car going over a cliff and he pushes so far into them that they stop wanting. And he's learned to take so much more from them, and so much more slowly, more completely, to take in ways so that they think they are giving what they didn't even know was theirs. No, he's not golden. Not brown. Something wild and green and growing and his hair rustles in the wind like new leaves whenever he enters the Ramble, resilient, the personification of spring in the truest sense of the word, how his being had been poured into this shape, not willed but cultivated by demented dimensions, poured and pouring, pouring into the mouths of sheepish accountants and retail clerks and mad garbage men and German tourists and drunk college boys following a rumor and memories of summers in the boat house, of older brothers showing them the ropes and the ropes are wet and thick with celestial seeds hanging off the chins of old men with monogrammed handkerchiefs and the presence of mind (and experience, forget the songs of experience, they crave the sighs) to put down a sheet of newspaper before kneeling so their wives won't question again the grass stains on their trousers.

From his apartment in the Time Warner Center overlooking the park, Golden Boy pulls an iPhone 6 Plus out of his Bathing Ape camouflage sweat pants pocket. He licks a finger to wipe away a smudge from his Nike SB X Diamond Dunks while looking at his phone —and wills his other hand to grow multiple spidery appendages so he can type and swipe faster; he has every app and multiple accounts and he knows how to be demure, to come on hard, to please, to tease, to entice. And once you're hooked he always types the same thing.

LOL let's meet in the park.

Some Nights in Kyoto

Some nights in Kyoto should never end. Ryouta smirked when an aunt, recently visiting from the countryside, had gushed breathlessly those very words upon returning from the theater. Now the sentiment all-too-painfully guttered within his stomach as the servants whisked their palanquin though lantern-strewn streets. The curtains were pulled back -night air wafted in as he rested his chin on the window sill. Outside steam rose from late night food stalls swamped by drunken merchants, drunker priests, and thirsty students hunched over one last bowl of soggy noodles. He couldn't stop thinking about the actor who played the character of Yoko, a courtesan who helps the ghost of her samurai lover exact revenge on the thieves who took his life.

As the palanquin bumped along, his father sat across from his son, toying with the netsuke of his tobacco pouch, small ivory toggles carved in the shape of happy bats, fangs stained brown from the constant fiddling of his fingertips -his habit whenever bemused or annoyed. He nestled back into his cushioned corner, content that such a rough and tumble boy would be so taken with a kabuki actor. It was all he and his wife could do to keep him out of the woods and clean in time for dinner, much less practice his Kanji; a crush on someone cultured and sophisticated would be a push in the right direction.

They turned onto a darker, quieter street. Ryouta's father off-handedly mentioned that, if the boy wanted, he could arrange for his son to meet the actor. Ryouta nodded rapidly and gave a quick "Hai!" in the affirmative, his attention already fixed on that future date, and the yet-to-be-selected gift he would give the kabuki actor in gratitude for his sublime existence. As they crossed the bridge that led to the family estate, the black waters below tumbled by like dying applause.

The next day, Ryouta and the family huntsman were in the woods that surrounded their estate. Spring had come early, and bright greenery sprouted in lively contrast to the still-dark, barren earth of the forest floor. They chanced upon a cherry tree in bloom, the first of the year. He pulled his knife out from its sharkskin hilt and cut the fullest branch. He had since learned the actor's name, Matsushima, as his father had sent a messenger to the actor, and an agreement had been made to have tea after tonight's performance. He learned that Matsushima was a year older than him and had spent time in Edo. Ryouta did not want the actor to think him unsophisticated, and had laid out his best kimono, planning to end his hunt early to bathe before dinner. The cherry blossoms would be a perfect present.

He let the huntsman carry his bow so he could better cradle the branch. The fragrant petals sang the song of an emerging season, all the better, for their perfume would sink into Matsushima's tatami mats. The actor would dream of him as he tossed and turned. . . He was surprised by his mother's voice. He hadn't even realized that they had reached home –he was so lost in thoughts of the coming night. She was supervising the maids as they scrubbed tatami mats and excitedly called him over.

"The first cherry blossoms of the season! This is beautiful, Ryouta. We can add the blossoms to the sweet tofu I was planning for dessert. How perfect." She lifted the branch out of his arms to examine the white buds, oblivious to how crushed her son was. He hung his head as he kicked off his sandals before the doorway. When he had restless nights and tossed his blanket aside, she would slip into his room and cover him. Winters, his mother would tap him quietly to let him know his father's bath was almost ready, so he could sneak in first and revel in the steeping water. As she held the branch up and turned it around to catch the light off the petals, he knew there was no way he could reclaim the blossoms. Dejected, he followed her inside, shoulders slumped.

At dinner, he was quiet, his mother cooing over the fresh mackerel, the jasmine rice, bringing up again and again the gift of the cherry blossoms, as if the arrow in Ryouta's heart needed to be ground deeper into the wound. Oblivious, his father had too much sake, as was his way when the nights warmed up. He sipped his nigori and observed his son's insincere politeness, how quickly he wolfed down his rice and only picked at the fish, typically his favorite meal. He motioned to his wife that the table should be cleared. As she rose, he tossed the boy a string thick with hollow coins and whispered, "If you leave now, you can stop by that street fair. I noticed one was setting up under the bridge by the playhouse. Get your new friend an interesting present there, but first rinse your mouth with some of this sake -no one wants to talk to someone stinking of mackerel."

Ryouta flushed and bowed deeply. Pocketing the money, he took a swig of alcohol and diligently swished it around. His mother returned with a servant to remove the remaining dishes as the boy scurried out of the room. His father tapped out some tobacco from his pouch and leaned back, satisfied that he had set his son on the path of good fortune.

Sweat dappled Ryouta's brow as the palanquin slowed

down; he hadn't realized how nervous he was until they crossed the bridge leading to the theater district. A white-faced geisha in a peach-colored kimono floated past as merchants hauling sacks of rice quietly forded the traffic. He rapped the ceiling, signaling the footmen to halt. He felt the weight of the coins in his satchel as he stepped from the palanquin. He was careful not to get his new sandals dusty and steered his way toward the box office. Beneath the bridge, a ragtag carnival had indeed set up.

Crowds had already formed in the streets before the theater, alluringly gold, awash in the glow of prematurely lit lanterns. When it was finally his turn to purchase a ticket, he was shocked to find that all the affordable seats were taken. He would have to spend most of his money on a box seat or wait out the performance, killing time in a noodle shop or by skipping stones at the river. A stout samurai huffed impatiently behind him, and Ryouta slid a stack of coins through the ticket seller's window.

The inside of the theater was dimly lit. Ryouta was alone in the box seats and found the roominess disquieting, but felt like a minor lord up there alone, and was pleased to see that the bow-legged samurai who'd rushed him at the ticket window hadn't been able to afford a ticket. Across the aisles below, women fanned themselves, not because it was too warm but rather to display new, expensive silk fans. He was shocked at how truncated the stage appeared. Over the curtain line, he could see the skeletal hints of other backdrops and weird machinations – which, rather than diminishing the magic of the theater, deepened his curiosity. That there were technical applications he'd not yet guessed at would give him and Matsushima something to talk about! After settling back in his seat, he began to worry that he'd spent too much money, that he wouldn't be able to afford the tea service and any dessert afterwards, but decided that he would simply order light and hope that Matsushima wasn't famished after a show. And then, suddenly, the lights dropped, and the performance commenced.

"Everything looks so different from up here!"

He surprised himself by talking out loud and reflexively covered his mouth, but he was still alone; no one else had purchased the other seats in his box. As the grieving Yoko, Matsushima once again shone, but from above he was a prostrate visage, his white kimono spilt across the stage as he mourned the death of his husband –from this angle the scene was reminiscent of one of the sensual and much handled woodblock prints of Utagawa Kuniyoshi that the huntsman liked to leer at when he was resting far from the household. He'd pull at his crotch and show them to Ryouta, who coveted every glance, a million questions forming in his mind, yet all he could do, trembling with the comics in his hand, was whisper "Hai!" over and over. He rubbed his sweaty palms across his thighs and tried once again to peer behind the curtain, to see around the corners at what makes things work.

After the show, they met at the back door of the theater, where Ryouta bowed perhaps a bit too formally and could feel Matsushima stiffen. Out of costume, the actor looked like any other boy he'd have encountered in the alleyways of Kyoto, though he was a bit lean –*did they not feed him enough to keep him womanly? Would he be starving and eat up my remaining coinage?* Ryouta quickly rose and gave a brief, comic shake, as if dismissing any sense of ceremony that could possibly exist between them, smiled, blurting out, "It's so great to see you again, and finally meet!"

They both laughed at his impetuousness and relaxed into a shared gait as they strolled toward the busy streets.

The boys stopped at a nearby teahouse, a popular gathering spot for students. Ryouta was surprised at how much they had in common and yet how different they were. He had boasted about how he'd hunted pheasant with a bow and arrow, only to have Matsushima explain that he'd had to learn both the bow and sword play in his theater training. Ghostly traces of white makeup clung to his hairline. Yet rather than act like a haughty star, the other boy was slyly humorous and polite – Ryouta tried to mimic his deft handling of the tea set, but burst out laughing after Matsushima told the story of how, as Yoko, during the scene where he mourned the death of his husband, the actor who played the corpse had not only fallen asleep but had begun to snore, so much so that the boy actor had to increase his wailing to match and mask the rhythmic sawing. Though they had only planned to meet for tea, the easy flow of their conversation naturally carried them back out into the meandering streets.

The theater district was alive with drunks, courtesans, boastful samurai, clinging couples, the scent of roasting skewers, and the lilting music from behind shoji screens. Ryouta recalled the small carnival and tugged at Matsushima's sleeve to follow- their fingers nearly interlocking. He was flush at the electricity of their first touch and clenched and unclenched his fists not knowing how to reconnect but badly wanting to.

Beneath the bridge, a throng of peasants, slumming nobles, and each and every class in between, all enthralled by treats sold and carnival games rigged. Crones ladled ridiculously cheap sake; hawkers plied sticky rainbows of candied fruit. To approaching revelers, it appeared as if the arch of the bridge simply caught and held the slow churn of steam and smoke from boiling dumplings and cooking fires, but the grey vapors were more than that. Some nights bleed into other realms, and certain nights and specific hours and dates allow for mysterious exchanges, and so within such crossroads the yokai set up shop. Strange creatures in human guise selling calamities and trickery: a gambling merchant might think he had won a fortune only to wake up and find his pockets filled with bits of dried squid instead of coin. Some yokai were formerly human beings, and these beings were especially cruel. A coquettish courtesan once purchased an exquisite powder at such a fair, the application of which provided undiminished beauty in the eyes of the beholder. In fact, many of her clients exclaimed that she looked years younger and possessed a certain glow. Yet every time she caught a glimpse of her own reflection in a mirror, all she saw was an outsized catfish in a kimono. Mostly harmless fun for otherworldly beings - this was a festive snare for all, with young lovers being especially susceptible.

As they moved with the crowd, Ryouta was relieved that their night was already a success. While Matsushima was practically hypnotized by a purple-robed magician's sleight of hand, he was able to study his face: his eyebrows went up in amazement with every trick, how his lips parted in a slight smile -the part of his kimono hinted at a bare chest that Ryouta wanted to see more of. Where the crowd thinned and the carnival petered out, long willows brushed the shore –he imagined pressing Matsushima against the shaded trunk of one such tree. The next stall was selling takoyaki, the small fried balls with morsels of octopus tucked within, which looked delicious. He could purchase some and invite Matsushima to share them by the river. . . His coin purse was empty, however. Crestfallen, he turned back to his date just as the magician finished his final trick with a flourish, disappearing behind a cloud of sulfuric smoke. The throng convulsed with applause, and as the old man who operated the stall coughed and wheezed. Ryouta impetuously palmed one of the octopus balls and pulled Matsushima away.

He led the other boy down by the river, arm across his shoulder in the same manner he'd seen samurai tumble out of a tavern, but there was a subtle difference in the way Matsushima leaned into his body that made Ryouta's heart pound. They stopped by the water's edge and, mimicking the magician's elaborate bow, he produced the takoyaki. Matsushima laughed, put his hands behind his back, and leaned down to eat it out of Ryouta's hand. They locked eyes as Matsushima's lips brushed his palm, and Ryouta wanted to kiss him then and there. But a strange look crossed Matsushima's eyes as he choked and spat the takoyaki out. Bringing his hands to his throat, he shook with a violent cough and fell to his knees. Ryouta panicked.

"Matsushima, my Matsushima! What's wrong?"

He knelt down and patted the sick boy's heaving back.

"Why, why?" Matsushima whispered, looking faint and confused as he gulped for breath.

Ryouta felt the ground for the takoyaki –it had turned into a dull, round stone, though he could feel the pitted area where Matsushima had taken a bite. Furious, he threw it into the river and roughly pulled the young actor to his feet.

"I've been tricked! We're going back to that carnival, and I'm going to beat that old man until he's blind."

They stumbled back toward the bridge. The crowd had since dwindled. The smoke had thickened and pulsed with a serpentine menace. The magician who had so astounded Matsushima stepped forward and yawned, then sloughed off his robe to reveal that he was actually an assemblage of giant, flesh-colored crickets stacked one atop the other. A geisha slowly folded the fan before her face and bowed toward them, her head one enormous, unblinking eye. However, all around, the people present moved about completely unaware. Ryouta gasped with fear. Matsushima, ill and oblivious, slumped further against him, and so he did his best to push on. Up ahead, the old man selling cursed morsels now had the face of a bemused tortoise, but instead of a tortoise's shell, his shoulders and back writhed with black hair that glistened like seaweed beneath midnight's moon.

He stood before the yokai and bowed deeply, severely.

"Please! Kind demon, I beg your forgiveness. Please! Make my friend well."

The old tortoise man stood still. A slight rustling noise emanated from his hairy shoulders, as if unseen creatures nested there.

Matsushima moaned, and Ryouta prostrated himself.

"Please! What is happening to my friend?"

"Why, he is becoming yokai," the old tortoise man murmured.

Ryouta looked up in terror.

"What? What can I do to stop this-please, please stop this!"

The yokai shrugged. "Simply return that which you stole before dawn, and all will be forgiven."

A gaggle of the creatures then began to dance and sing nonsense songs around the boys. Ryouta pulled Matsushima through the remaining throng of unsuspecting humans and weird monsters down to the river's edge.

The river was tranquil. Matsushima was listless, his face pale, eyes unfocused, flesh powdery, viridescent. His eyebrows had begun to extend upward like the antennae of a moth; the transformation into a yokai had begun. Ryouta gave him a gentle squeeze and lowered his limp form onto the rocky beach.

The riverbed stretched in every direction, an expanse of dull, round stones.

Ryouta slipped out of his sandals and stepped into the cold, apathetic water, and tried to discern from the moon's position just how many hours were left before sunrise.

Grimly, he thought, *some nights in Kyoto should never end.*

Essay: Recall the Creature: My Introduction to Horror and Queerness

Every Saturday before noon, I would nestle my buttocks into the tough fibers of the blue and green Sargasso Sea of shag carpet that stretched before the television in our darkened family room. The imaginary waves of this emerald ocean had drowned a menagerie of Micronauts and assorted action figures pitted against each other in battles that crossed trademarked boundaries galore. These playful waters froze, however, once the antecedent episode of Star Trek zipped away into a nebula of reruns. *Creature Feature* announced itself with an eerie blast of organ music, a swirl of classic movie monster images, and Dr. Paul Bearer appeared to present that afternoon's horror film.

Dr. Paul Bearer single-handedly introduced me to my childhood heroes: Dracula, Frankenstein, the Wolfman, the Mummy and, importantly, the Creature from the Black Lagoon. The Creature from the Black Lagoon was significant as I grew up in Florida, in a coastal town parceled out by far-reaching canals to increase the amount of water front property available, allowing alligators to slip into peaceful swimming pools at night, driving neighborhood dogs wild. The Creature was a Florida monster. Though the story took place in the Amazon, I knew that it was filmed in Florida. I recognized the Spanish moss and the swamp from family canoe trips to Myakka River State

Park. This was a monster in reach. Looming over all of them, however, was Godzilla. This behemoth mirrored my nuclear fears as Reagan swaggered onto the world stage. As a child, I would have my parents bring home all of the empty boxes from work. I'd take them to our neighbor's Florida room, basically a large, screened in porch, and erect a city. Streets filled with matchbox cars, windows and bricks drawn on the cardboard. Once I had a suitable metropolis, I'd roar my best Godzilla roar and lay waste to all that I had assembled. As Andrew Cunanan quoted in his senior year book, "Après mois le déluge." *After me, destruction.*

Every week Dr. Paul Bearer ushered monsters into my home. His oddly reassuring death-rattle voice spat out tidbits of film lore with bad puns and the promise of more gore after a brief commercial break. He shambled about the cardboard set like a disheveled undertaker, greasy straight hair parted down the middle, not quite dead but waning and profane nonetheless. And the range of the movies shown on *Creature Feature* was monstrously wide, from Hammer classics to schlocky atomic-age drive-in drivel. Nearly every monster marched through the halls of *Creature Feature*, exquisite classics, from the Japanese film *Matango* (*Godzilla* director Ishiro Honda, 1963) dubbed and re-titled *Attack of the Mushroom People* for U.S. release, this atmospheric masterpiece features shipwrecked folk battling hunger and a horde of humanoid fungus to the then-nearly contemporary film *Don't Be Afraid of the Dark* (dir. John Newland, 1973) where miniature creatures stalked a young woman in her house. Its unforgettable ending terrified me as a child but I'd watch it whenever it came on. This was a made-for-TV horror film, a now nearly forgotten 70s sub-genre that gave Steven Spielberg his start with *Duel* (1971), about a relentless, murderous truck and a personal favorite, *Gargoyles* (Bill Norton 1972), with beautiful creature effects from Stan Winston, who went on to win Academy Awards for the James Cameron films *Aliens* (1986), *Terminator 2: Judgement Day* (1991), and *Jurassic*

Park (dir. Spielberg, 1993).

1950s America was well-represented, with the hormonal *I Was a Teenage Werewolf* (dir. Gene Fowler Jr., 1957) and identity crisis freak-out *I Was a Teenage Frankenstein* (dir. Herbert L. Stock, 1957) both in glorious black and white. Also presented: several irradiated homeland beasts that could give Godzilla a run for his money, *The Amazing Colossal Man* (dir. Bert I. Gordon, 1957), *The Deadly Mantis* (dir. Nathan Juran, 1957) and *Attack of the 50 Foot Woman* (dir. Nathan Juran, 1958).

Dr. Paul Bearer served as my celluloid Virgil, leading me through the various circles of the horror universe, where misunderstood monsters lurked, powerful outcasts that just wanted to be left alone, all fueled my imagination and a profoundly nascent understanding (and yearning for) camp. I was being given metaphors to better interpret and navigate a community in opposition to my existence. When I was in middle school it became public knowledge that two twin boys, about my age, both hemophiliacs, were HIV positive. Soon afterwards, someone set their house on fire and the family fled town. I thought of the villagers in the Frankenstein movies. This town that I loved and had nurtured me suddenly expanded to include dark, previously unknown avenues where neighbors hunted neighbors. Before I comprehended that I was gay, I knew I was somehow unsafe.

Dr. Paul Bearer hosted *Creature Feature* from 1973 until his death in 1995. Digging around online, I've learned that he got his start on television in the 60s as another character, Count Shockula, on a North Carolina station. There he adopted his Dr. Paul Bearer identity and relocated to Saint Petersburg, Florida. My nearby hometown, Sarasota, served as the winter headquarters for the Ringling Bros. and Barnum & Bailey Circus. To better integrate themselves into the town, they set up a circus for the local children, which thrives to this day and where I spent my later-elementary and middle school years as a clown and unicyclist. We occasionally performed in other towns or marched in local parades, and during one such parade, I actually saw Dr. Paul Bearer. He was talking to a local female newscaster. I approached without any intent to engage - I didn't have any questions or clever things to say, I just wanted to be near -to step into the shadow of his cape. His voice was *normal*, flirty, out-of-character. I was shocked and sulked away, having had no idea that his act was *an* act, that he was playing a character much like I was a clown but only when I donned the make-up and rubber nose. I'd just never seen someone drop their mask before to realize we all wear one.

This dark menagerie of film monsters was the polar opposite of the world I was born into: football and boy scouts, camping and fishing, my obsession was tolerated with bemusement, but for me a door had opened: I scoured movie ads in the local newspaper for new horror releases and since they were rated R, I would read the novelizations, devouring Alan Dean Foster's *Aliens*, Dean Koontz, *The Funhouse*, and the like in bed at night. I caught a commercial for *Dawn of the Dead* once, and was so hypnotized that I watched hours of television hoping to again catch sight of zombies in a shopping mall. Of course, I first saw *Night of the Living Dead* (dir. Romero, 1968) on *Creature Feature*, and when independent video stores started popping up, I finally rented the sequels. My hometown gets a shout out in the opening scene of *Day of the Dead* (dir. Romero, 1985), which is set in South Florida; its images of the apocalypse brought directly to my shores thrilled me beyond belief.

Creature Feature also served as my introduction to Egar Allen Poe with *The Raven* (dir. Corman, 1963) and *Pit and the Pendulum* (Corman, 1961) in turn leading to a life-long fascination with the oeuvre of Vincent Price. Many of his films were *Creature Feature* mainstays (though oddly not *The Abominable Dr. Phibes* or its admirable sequel *Dr. Phibes Rises Again* (dir. Robert Fuest 1971, 1972). Maybe the good Dr. Paul Bearer thought there should only be one physician in the house?). With every hypnotic, prancing performance by

Vincent Price, from staking the vampire hordes of *The Last Man on Earth* (dir. Ublado Ragona, 1964) or seeking Shakespearean revenge in *Theater of Blood* (dir. Douglas Hickox, 1973), I sunk deeper into camp quicksand. And not all of the films were horror. I was introduced to the Greek myths via the wondrous and nimble creations of Ray *Harryhausen* in *Jason and the Argonauts* (dir. John Chaffey, 1963). I was also turned me on to science fiction classics like *The Day the Earth Stood Still* (Robert Wise, 1951), and the original *Invasion of the Body Snatchers* (dir. Don Siegel, 1956).

Dr. Paul Bearer so singularly belonged to me that, as an adult, I was shocked to discover there was an entire army of such ghouls that populated American airtime. Regional witches and zombified hosts monopolizing local markets, earning the affection and fascination of other outcast kids who grew up in that era -there's even a documentary about this cultural phenomenon: *American Scary* (dir. John E. Hudgens, 2006). Certainly Elvira, Mistress of the Dark, has risen to the top, from hosting locally in Los Angeles to becoming a queer icon and national figure with a movie and Funko POPs in her likeness. Vampira started all this horror business back in 1954. I first saw Vampira in Ed Wood's infamous *Plan 9 from Outer Space* (1959) on *Creature Feature*. But Dr. Paul Bearer belongs to me. And to be clear, he didn't recruit me. One of my earliest memories is being at The Pirates of the Caribbean ride at Disney World with my family and seeing a skull ring made of brass. This shiny death's head hypnotized me and I demanded it with all the fury a small child could muster. I was granted my wish, even though the ring was much too big to wear. I was okay with that; I knew I would grow into it someday.

Recall the Creature, which is how fans of *The Creature from the Black Lagoon* (dir. Jack Arnold, 1954) refer to the monster. That or the Gill-Man. The movie, and, it should be noted, the only wholly American creation in the Universal Studio monster stable -the others having their basis in European literature and mythology, was such a success that it spawned two sequels: *Revenge of the Creature* (dir. Jack Arnold, 1956), set in a Florida marine park and featuring a skinny Clint Eastwood in his cinematic debut and *The Creature Walks Among Us* (dir. John Sherwood, 1956). In each film sympathy lies with the Creature. As a little boy, I swam the same murky waters as this aquatic monster. I wandered the irradiated ruins of Tokyo and slunk through the shadows of Carfax Abbey. Later, while reading Edgar Rice Burroughs novels as a pre-teen, I realized I wanted to be a writer. The primeval ink of my imagination, however, is drawn from those first electric images of tantalizing horror, and the preternatural sense that I wasn't the one who needed rescuing.

About the Author

Tom Cardamone is the editor of *Crashing Cathedrals: Edmund White by the Book* and is the author of the Lambda Literary Award-winning speculative novella *Green Thumb* as well as the erotic fantasy *The Lurid Sea* and other works of fiction. Additionally, he has edited *The Lost Library: Gay Fiction Rediscovered* and co-edited *Fever Spores: The Queer Reclamation of William S. Burroughs*.

He co-curates The Library of Homosexual Congress, an imprint of Rebel Satori Press, which preserves and promotes classic and provocative works of gay literature and nonfiction, with a focus on the AIDS crisis, the nascent gay rights movement, as well as irreverent works of sexual culture and groundbreaking titles that deserve renewed attention.